This is a work of fiction. Similarities to real people, places, or events are entirely coincidental.

THE DEVIL'S DUNGEON

First edition. October 23, 2023.

Copyright © 2023 Cassie Smith.

ISBN: 979-8223861591

Written by Cassie Smith.

DEDICATION

To my spouse for always supporting me, encouraging me, and being by my side with everything that I do. To my sister Erin, my sister-in-law Hope and my brother Leland for being my biggest cheerleaders while writing this story. To my parents for always being the biggest supporters and encouragers of my dreams. Lastly, to Wamingo Publishing, LLC for supporting me and publishing my first short story and allowing me to go rogue.

The Devil's Dungeon
Written by Cassie Smith

<u>**Prologue-1964**</u>

At age fifteen, Helena had experience far beyond her years. She excelled at school, always getting perfect grades. At fourteen, she graduated high school. One of the youngest in her home city of Portland, Oregon to do so. Despite Helena's intelligence, her favorite courses weren't academic but sports. She loved to run cross country and had won many medals for her agility and swiftness.

When she was a child, her aunt was granted guardianship of her due to her parents alcohol and drug abuse. She never saw her parents again, but she didn't care. Her aunt was a much better guardian anyway. She taught her how to cook and clean, and even some basic car maintenance skills. Helena had lived with her aunt for nearly five years; but her aunt was old with a bad heart and passed away before her fifteenth birthday.

On the day of her aunt's funeral, Helena decided to run away to avoid Child Protective Services. She fled in tears, not knowing what she was going to do or where she would go so long as it was somewhere far from the empty house that now awaited her.

She had no idea how long she ran. It could have been hours, or it could have been days. But when she stopped, it wasn't due to exhaustion but because of a strange cabin she happened upon in the pre-dusk gloom. It was a rickety old thing that sat out in the middle of nowhere, surrounded by trees. By the looks of the place, nobody had been in residence for some time.

Helena walked up the front stairs, which were worn and withered and creaked with every step she took. She paused on the small porch. Its planking looked just as rotten as the stairs, so she tested her weight before proceeding for fear the wood would crumble underneath her. Once satisfied the planking would hold, she continued to the front door and knocked.

No one answered. She knocked again and this time the door swung inward on its own. Helena was disturbed by this, but she was also cold and hungry. Night was falling, and she had no intention of sleeping out under the stars.

She asked if anybody was home, shakily at first, but when no one answered her voice rose in confidence. Certain the cabin was abandoned, Helena stepped inside and looked around. The place was empty save for a couch, a fireplace with wood next to the hearth, and a small kitchen with a little round table next to it. As she crept further inside, she saw a couple of abstract paintings hanging on the wall in the living room. The cabin seemed quaint, but ancient. The wood paneling on the walls was withered and oxidized. She looked to her left and saw a long narrow hallway. After walking down it and through a mass of cobwebs, she discovered a door which, upon opening, revealed a large bedroom.

She stepped inside. To her right was an antique dresser with a large mirror and six drawers, three on each side of the dresser. Directly in front of her was a king size four-poster bed with a down comforter on it. To her left was a bathroom with a spa tub and a small shower. She made her way from the large bedroom and walked across the hallway to what looked like a little girl's bedroom.

Beside it sat another bedroom that looked identical to the master bedroom except for the lack of a bathroom and a twin mattress instead of a king for the bed. The bathroom here was located across the hall and featured a grotesque looking pink and red tile floor, a gaudy red toilet, and a hot pink shower curtain. Helena looked away in disgust. The garish over-decoration was too much for her senses. She wondered if the decorator was high when they worked on this room.

She saw a closed door at the far left hand side of the hallway and walked over to it. She tried the knob. It turned in her hand, but the door wouldn't budge. She forced it open with her shoulder and stared down a long wooden staircase that led into utter darkness.

Helena got a sinister feeling as she stared into that dark abyss. Could there be somebody down there, like the cabin's owners maybe? It wouldn't hurt to go down and check, at least let them know she wasn't a burglar. Then again, maybe nobody was home. Maybe this was like one of those summer cabins where people only came to stay a few months out of the year.

She searched for a wall switch but couldn't find one. The realization brought relief. She didn't see any kind of light bulb and she didn't have a flashlight handy. There was no way she was going to try exploring that ominous basement in the dark. No, best to wait until morning. At least then the place wouldn't feel so spooky.

Helena walked back down the hallway to the kitchen. She searched for non-expired food in the fridge and found some grape jelly, some yellow government cheese, and a few condiments. She had better luck in the pantry, where the canned soups and easy-bake items were stored. Her stomach rumbled but she dared not eat yet. She decided that if the place truly was empty then she would hide out here for a while. But first, she had to be sure she was alone.

Helena sat in the living room for a bit, listening for any sign of the cabin's owners. This soon grew tiresome and she grabbed a book off a shelf to keep herself occupied. It grew dark outside, and after a couple of hours of waiting, she reached two conclusions. First: nobody was home. Second: nobody was coming home, at least not tonight.

Feeling better, she took some cheese from the fridge and found some crackers in the pantry. With a thankful sigh, she sat at the kitchen table and allowed herself the luxury of a late dinner, such as it was.

She looked around, noting the layers of dust and cobwebs that adorned the shelves and furnishings. If not for the food in the refrigerator she would have thought the place abandoned. Maybe it's a hideout, Helena mused. Like in those gangster films her dad liked to get high to. She went to the hearth in the living room and contemplated gathering wood for a fire. After a moment's indecisiveness, she decided against it. She wanted the warmth, but the smoke might draw the wrong kind of attention. Instead, she went to the master bedroom at the back of the cabin and settled into the biggest bed she'd ever seen. She fell asleep instantly.

Helena woke at first light. She used the adjoining bathroom and then made her way to

the kitchen, being sure to keep an eye out for the owners or any fellow transients along the

way. Once positive she was alone, Helena breathed a sigh of relief and rummaged in the fridge for breakfast. She found half a carton of eggs and checked them for a date. She couldn't find one, but they smelled fine, so she decided to chance it. After a brief search for a pan she made herself scrambled eggs, adding in the last of the government cheese for texture. There was no bacon, but she made due with a half-empty bag of jerky she found in the pantry.

Once all was ready, she settled on the couch in the living room and contemplated her situation while she scarfed down the contents of her plate (she didn't realize until that minute how ravenous she was). Helena knew she couldn't stay here forever but she didn't want to keep running either. She wanted a home of her own, some place where she belonged. Who knew, if she was careful maybe she could stay here. It had been twenty-four hours already and there was still no sign of the cabin's owners.

Still, doubt remained. Someone had bought those eggs she ate. As well as paid for the electricity that powered the fridge where she had found said eggs. Was that person gone for only a short time? Were they on vacation? Were they in a car accident and were now residing at the local morgue?

Helena decided to take each day as it came, at least for the time being. Today she was going to explore the basement. If all went well with that then she would contemplate her next move.

Helena found a flashlight in a utility drawer in the kitchen and went to the edge of the basement stairs. She was a little apprehensive about going down there, but she convinced herself that there was nothing to be afraid of. If there was somebody hiding in the basement she was sure she would've heard them mucking about last night. And it wasn't like there were ghosts down there, that was just crazy. Such things didn't exist outside of books and movies. So what was there to be afraid of?

Slowly, she made her way down the stairs. The amber glow of her flashlight cut a swath through the darkness. Helena moved the beam back and forth, studying every nook and cranny. She paused at the bottom and took in her surroundings. The basement was enormous. She trained her flashlight on a passage to her left and turned down it.

The floor was primarily dirt and bumpy in places. She stumbled once and cut her palm on a nail in the wall when she reached out to balance herself. After that, she divided her attention between the passage and the floor to avoid another accident. She shined the light on the cement walls, which looked as if they had been painted white. She found this strange seeing as how the rest of the basement looked uncared for.

Helena continued down the passage, a little more wary now. By this point, she must have walked the length of the cabin and then some. Just how far did this basement extend?

To her right, she saw the outline of a door in the darkness. She flashed her light inside and saw an empty room with an old clawfoot bathtub in its center. The tub was pretty rusty and it looked like it hadn't been used in many years. She thought it was a little eerie. Helena continued walking. She wondered how far she was from the cabin now. It seemed as if this passage went on forever. She looked to her right and saw a blue door that resembled something straight out of Alice In Wonderland.

The door was short, no more than four feet tall, and appeared just wide enough for her to squeeze through. What was such a tiny door doing all the way down here? It looked newer than anything else in the basement, as if someone had just recently built it. She walked slowly to the door and tried the knob. It turned in her hand and the door opened slightly but became stuck midway. She pressed against it, having to use all her strength, until the door gave and she was able to enter.

Inside she saw a narrow plank, which led to a spiral staircase that wound its way down into absolute darkness. This was getting stranger by the minute. She navigated the rickety plank and felt a sense of relief when she made it to the staircase. She wondered if she should risk going down and then gave a mental shrug. Why not? She'd already come this far, might as well go for broke.

Helena started down the stairs. Time seemed to stand still as she descended deeper and deeper into the bowls of this mysterious place. She had no idea how long she walked but she eventually came to another door. Helena tried the knob but it wouldn't turn. You've got to be kidding, she thought. All that walking only to reach a door that won't open.

Helena was very curious now. She ran back up the stairs (strangely, they didn't seem as long this time around), across the plank, and through the open door at the top. Helena took a moment to catch her breath and then decided to try the other side of the basement.

She made her way back to the main staircase. Once there, she began down the right passage. It looked pretty much the same as the left side except here there were more dirt hills. These were covered with cinderblocks. Helena found the sight intriguing. In her current frame of mind, she wondered if the cinder blocks were put there to keep something buried under the dirt.

She shuddered at the thought and quickly dismissed it as she concentrated on the task at hand. She continued down the passage until she came to another room. Peering inside, she found shackles hanging from the ceiling and an old rusted cart that looked like something they laid bodies on in a funeral home. She moved on from that room in a hurry.

To her left she saw another door. This one opened onto a room with a plank that led to a spiral staircase. It was nearly identical to the other room. So much so that she at first thought she had gone full circle. But the staircase here had *fleur de lis* carvings in its railing where the other had none. She walked across the plank to the staircase and began down it. At the bottom, which, much like the first, seemed to take forever to get to, she found another door. This time, however, the door opened.

The room inside was massive. She stepped through the doorway and stared up at the ceiling, her mouth agape. A gigantic chandelier hung above her, its light reflecting off the white stone walls and revealing yet another staircase that led up to what seemed like many more rooms. She continued to walk through the cavernous space, so huge it seemed almost like an underground castle. She wondered how all of this had gotten here. Did someone actually take the time and trouble (not to mention money) to build it? Was it something that someone worked really hard to bury? Just where the heck was she?

The Reverie mental hospital wasn't far from here. She wondered if maybe these passages led under the hospital. Maybe it had been built as a place for its patients to hang out between treatments. Helena laughed at herself. That was just silly. Still, she had no idea how any of this was possible, but it was so cool! She had discovered something truly amazing. The floors were marble and the place looked immaculate. Unlike the rest of the basement, or cabin for that matter, it seemed that someone had gone to great lengths to keep this place clean.

She started to look around but didn't get too far before she ran into someone. She looked up, terrified, at a tall man dressed in a black tuxedo with a bow tie. He had piercing blue eyes and neatly combed black hair. Helena wanted to run back the way she had come, but she gathered her courage and in a deep breath said, "Oh, sir. Excuse me! I'm so sorry! I didn't . . . I mean . . . I was just exploring; I . . . I apologize. I didn't know anyone was down here."

The man smiled at her. "Oh, you've found us! That's wonderful. We've been waiting for you."

"Me?" Wonder overcame Helena's suspicion.

"Oh yes," the man said, reaching for her. "We've been waiting for you for a very long time."

Chapter One

Some Years Later . . .

There were always three girls. When one disappeared, another would show up to take her place. None of them were told where the new arrivals came from, though they suspected they were caught in the same manner they had been. They learned not to ask too many questions. At fifteen, the girls were little more than children, and as such, they were more susceptible to authority. Questions often led to punishment and that was something the girls learned very quickly to fear.

The girls remained captives of the woman they came to know as the "Madame" only so long as they managed to stay alive. The lucky ones died within a month, others remained captives for a year or more. No one ever escaped the Madame's clutches.

That is, until one night towards the end of summer when the impossible—or at least, what most thought impossible—happened.

Boston, Massachusetts . . .

Megan's family was very well off. She had a seven bedroom, four bathroom house. Her cheerleader status allowed her to like and dislike whoever she wanted. She was a goody two shoes according to her parents. However, when they went out of town Megan would always have pool parties at the house in their four-acre backyard, which, with its two water slides and lazy river, resembled a water park in all but name.

Her parents had a loving relationship and spent their free time alone together. Megan seemed more of an afterthought. They didn't spend much time with her and when they did, they were all over each other instead of paying attention to her. She wasn't entirely sure why they bothered having her if they didn't want her in their lives.

It had been like that as long as Megan could remember. She swore to herself that if she had kids, she was going to devote her whole life to them and make sure that they were happy and knew she was their mom.

On the day Megan was taken, she was walking home from school via the same route she always took. Her mom always said she had to keep out of the alleys and stay around people and stores. It was only three blocks home, but one could never be too careful.

She had a boyfriend named Alex. He was captain of the school's football team. They had been together a total of six months. She and Alex were very happy and everyone at school was jealous of their relationship. Megan liked it that way because that meant she was in the spotlight all the time. She had never been with any guy longer than Alex and she felt like she was falling hard for him.

On this particular day as she walked home from cheerleading practice, she noticed an unmarked white van driving slowly down the street opposite her. Megan didn't feel as if she was being followed, but she moved closer to the shops and quickened her pace just the same.

All at once, she heard the van door slide open, followed by the sound of feet hitting the pavement. She half-turned and saw a large, beefy man dressed in a white uniform bearing down on her. She started to run, but she was no match for her pursuer. His left hand, rough and calloused, grabbed her from behind. The right placed a cloth over her nose and mouth. It smelled funny and the more she inhaled the harder it became to resist. The next thing she knew, she was being thrown in the back of the white van. Within seconds of that, she fell unconscious.

When she came to, she saw a man sitting in front of her. She closed her eyes quickly so that he wouldn't see she was awake. They were driving along the road for what felt like an eternity. Finally, the van stopped and she heard voices.

"Still looks like she's out; I'll carry her.

Megan felt the same rough hands as before grab her by the arms and throw her over one wide shoulder. She dared not open her eyes as the beefy man carried her along, but she could tell they entered a building first by the sound of a door opening and shutting and then by the change in atmosphere as the steady breeze of the summer evening gave way to the sterility of an enclosed space.

She felt herself carried down a set of stairs. She risked opening one eye ever so slightly for a peek at her surroundings; her vision was hazy from whatever she'd been drugged with and she had a hard time focusing on anything, but she definitely saw stairs. Lots and lots of stairs, spiraling down who knew how many floors. It was immensely dark wherever they were, and the only thing she could make out was a beam of light from a flashlight in her kidnapper's hand. She closed her eye so as not to risk being seen awake. In doing so, she fell unconscious again.

When Megan next woke, she found herself alone in a dark room. She shivered against the cold as she slowly got to her feet. She didn't know where she was. It was so dark she couldn't even see her hand in front of her face.

"Hello?" she yelled. Only the echo of her voice replied. She held her hands in front of her and walked forward. She felt dizzy, but she didn't fall down. She counted fifteen steps before her hands touched what felt like a concrete wall. She made her way left, dragging her fingers along the wall. After five steps, she came to a smooth surface in the wall that must have been a door. She ran her hands down the door until she came to a knob. She tried to turn it, but it was locked tight.

Megan continued to feel her way along the wall. From what she could tell, she was in a small square-shaped room. Her fingers tore through a cobweb. "Eeee!" she squeaked and quickly put her hand over her mouth for fear that someone was there and would make fun of her for her girly outburst.

Farther along, her searching hands slid up the wall slightly and felt the bottom part of a window. It was too high to try opening, but come morning maybe she might have enough light to see by.

Megan continued on until she reached the fourth corner of the room. Having completed her search with nothing to show for it but a locked door and a window she couldn't reach, she slid down against the wall, put her face in her hands, and tried not to cry.

A few days later in Raleigh, NC . . .

Abigail, or "Abby" to her friends, grew up in Raleigh, North Carolina. She loved the city. As far as she was concerned, it was one of the best places in the country to live. She loved the beach. It wasn't very far from her house and one of her fondest childhood memories was picnicking along the shore with her parents, playing in the sand, building sandcastles, and jumping in the waves.

She was an only child and glad that her parents decided to keep it that way. To say that her parents spoiled her rotten was an understatement. They pretty much gave her whatever she wanted. Her favorite thing she owned was her trampoline. Whenever she jumped on it, she felt free, like a bird soaring toward the heavens.

Abby was incredibly intelligent despite being a spoiled brat. She skipped both the fourth and fifth grade because she was already ahead of her classmates in maturity and academics. She loved to read, her favorite genres being psychological thrillers and nonfiction. At fifteen, Abby was a blossoming teenager. She had natural red hair and bright green eyes, she was on the swim team and the best swimmer in her school.

The day of her abduction started like any other. She had finished swim practice and was starting her mile walk home. She noticed a white, windowless van driving slowly in the direction she was going. She didn't really think much of it because she'd been taking this same route since freshman year without any trouble. She said hello to the Tibetan shop owner standing outside his store, slowly drawing on a cigarette. The gentleman waved to her in response.

Had Abby remained on her usual path she may well have been okay, but she decided to take a shortcut through the side streets because she knew her mom had made strawberry rhubarb pie that afternoon and she couldn't wait to get home and eat some. On rhubarb pie days, mom always let her eat dessert before dinner no ifs, ands, or buts.

She cut through the shops to the next street over. As she was getting ready to turn onto her home street, she noticed the strange white van again. That can't be the same one, she thought. But then, how many windowless vans were around here?

Abby started to walk faster. She heard something that sounded like a van door sliding open. It was followed by heavy footsteps coming up quick behind her. She started running. Had she been the star of the track team instead of the swim team she might have made it, but as it was, she couldn't outpace her pursuer. Large hands grabbed her and a cloth covered her mouth before she could scream. She immediately passed out.

It was some time before Abby woke. When she came to she saw she was in a small room lit by a tiny window. In the corner opposite her, she saw a girl with her head resting in her lap.

"Hello?" she whispered.

Startled, Megan looked up. She stared at Abby, noting first her bright red hair, which stood out in the thin shaft of light like a field on fire.

"Hello," said Megan.

"What is this place?" asked Abby.

"How the hell should I know," Megan said. "I've been here for what feels like days and I haven't seen anyone."

Abby took that as a cue to shut her mouth.

Why does that girl have to be so mean? She thought.

A couple days later in Miami, Florida . . .

Summer Durth was a troublemaker. She'd been arrested a few times for underage drinking, but she never did drugs, that was her parents thing. She cherished her alcohol, though. She loved video games, comic books, music, and parties as well. Summer was the most popular of the goth kids in her school. She dyed her hair black, all her clothes were black, and her beautiful blue eyes were accentuated by black makeup.

Those who knew Summer couldn't understand why she chose to hang around the goth kids, because under all those baggy clothes and chains, she was gorgeous. Everyone speculated that it was a boy she had previously dated that turned her on to the lifestyle. She left such speculation to people's imaginations. The fact of the matter was, she dressed the way she did to ward off conversation from those she had no desire to talk to. No one knew about her parents, and how badly she needed to get out of the house sometimes. Her fake I.D. got her into all the clubs she wanted whenever she needed to unwind and drink the night away.

On this particular day, she was watching the clock at school, waiting for the final bell to ring.

Tick tock, tick tock . . .

She hated these days where an hour felt like a day and the day itself went on for an eternity. Finally, when she felt she couldn't take it any longer, the bell rang. She hurried to her locker and threw everything inside; homework wasn't happening tonight, no way. She was going to a rave with Jacob. Summer really liked him even though they'd only been dating for three months. The two of them were a good match.

Summer made her way out the school doors and into the sticky weather of mid-August. She found Jacob waiting for her by the bike rack, dressed in a black T-shirt and jeans, a cigarette dangling from the corner of his thin lips. He reminded her of a young Morrissey.

"Hey beautiful," he said in way of greeting. Summer wrapped her arms around his shoulders and kissed him hard on the mouth. She couldn't wait until the weather got cooler. All this black was sweltering, but when she wore it, people left her alone. She hated dripping sweat the second she walked outside, especially when she was with her boyfriend.

Jacob only lived a block away from her house, but he always walked her halfway. They arrived at his place first and he kissed her goodbye. "See you in a bit, babe," he said and headed inside to the sound of his mom calling for him to hurry up and take out the garbage.

She received no such greeting from her parents. As usual, she found her mom and dad lying on the couch, oblivious to their surroundings. She could tell by the way they were talking that they were high. They seemed to get stoned every day and teachers and authority figures expected her to take an interest in something "useful." If her parents wouldn't, why should she?

Summer ran upstairs to get ready for the party. An hour later, she stepped out the front door and locked her oblivious parents inside. She made her way quickly down the block to Jacob's house. Despite her tough girl façade, she didn't like walking around at night by herself. Summer had just passed the Crawford's house on the corner when she noticed a white unmarked van idling ahead of her. As she began to pass it, one of the doors flew open.

"Hey, girl with all the chains. Come here."

Summer jumped and began to back away from the van as a tall, rough-looking man climbed out of it.

"Who, me?" she asked.

"Yeah. Who else would I be talking to?" the man said. Summer looked around, but there was no one else on the street.

"No way," Summer said. She started to run and heard the man do the same. Panicking now, she tried to pick up her pace but the man grabbed her from behind.

Summer remembered some fighting moves she'd seen on television and tried to hit the man in the jaw with her elbow but missed. The guy actually laughed at her. Summer kicked her legs wildly and managed to connect with the guy's groin. He let go of her and fell hard on his knees.

"You bitch!" he yelled.

Summer started to run again. If she could just get to Jacob's house, she'd be safe. She heard the heavy footsteps pick up. Then she felt something hard hit her in the head. She crumbled to the ground.

"Teach you to fight me."

They were the last words she heard before the world grew dark.

Chapter 2

Back in the dark room, Megan and Abby still weren't speaking to each other. Abby was trying to think of something to say that might break the ice when the door swung open and a tall, mean-looking oaf threw another girl into the room. He slammed the door shut again before the new arrival even hit the floor.

Summer had no idea how long she was out, but when she opened her eyes, she saw two girls around her age sitting in the dark. Neither said a word as they turned and stared at her. She decided to say something before the silence drove her nuts. "What the hell is this place?"

For a moment, she thought neither of them were going to answer, but Abby responded with a petulant, "I don't know."

Summer looked next to Megan, who continued to stare blankly at her. "What's your problem?" Summer demanded. Megan didn't bother with a reply, just shifted her gaze back to the walls again. Abby, however, found her feet and walked over to her.

"Name's Abby. What's yours?" she said, sitting next to Summer.

"What's it to you?" Summer said.

"Well, nothing really, but I thought since we're in this room together and we've clearly been kidnapped or something, then maybe we should work together to get out."

"Yeah, well, I got news for you both. I don't need your help to get out of here. I can manage just fine on my own."

Megan piped in with: "Yeah, and just how do you plan on doing that? You think we haven't already tried escaping? The door is locked and the window is too high to climb out of."

Summer walked to the door and tried to open it but the knob wouldn't turn. She kicked the door hard but all that accomplished was a hurt toe.

"Told you," Megan said.

Undaunted, Summer reached for the knob again, meaning to rend it from the woodwork if need be, but the knob turned on its own, causing her to jump back with a start.

A woman with curly red hair that stuck up every which way entered, holding a lantern before her. She wore a dress that Summer thought resembled a slip. Abby studied the woman's face, noting with distaste that she really needed somebody to help her with her makeup, which looked as if it was applied with a paint roller.

"Oh, hello ladies!" the woman crooned. "I see you're all awake. That's perfect. Welcome to the dungeon. I'm sure you're all wondering why you're here. Let's get you all to your own separate rooms. So many fun surprises in your futures!"

The girls' shocked disbelief melted away and they surrounded the woman, questioning and arguing with her at the same time.

"No way!" said Summer.

"I'm not going anywhere with you," Abby chimed in.

"Who are you anyway?" Megan demanded.

The woman didn't answer. Instead, she grabbed Abby, who stood nearest her, by the collar of her shirt. Abby shrieked and bit her hand. The woman slapped Abby on the side of the head to make her let go. "Okay, I can tell this will be a bit harder than I thought," she said, studying the bite mark between the web of her thumb and forefinger.

A large beefy man appeared in the doorway behind the woman. Summer recognized him as the one who had hit her on the head. He reached for Abby, who lashed out at him with hands like talons, but he side-stepped her easily and put a wet cloth over her mouth. Within seconds, Abby fell silent.

Summer realized she was next. The man approached her, grinning in his self-assured dominance over her. But Megan sprinted for him and, before the woman could utter a word of warning, she was on his back, nails digging into his doughy face. The man threw her off him with a grunt of pain and the woman grabbed her by the arms before she could retaliate.

"Hurry up!" she hissed at the goon.

Summer made for the open door, but the goon grabbed a fistful of her hair and held the cloth over her face until she stopped kicking.

He turned next to Megan, who struggled to free herself from the woman's clutches, but her hands were held behind her back, making it impossible to maneuver. The man put the cloth over her mouth and she fell unconscious.

When she finally opened her eyes, Megan found herself lying on a cold table in a dimly lit room. She couldn't move her arms or legs. Her head pounded something awful. Her wrists and ankles were secured firmly to the table by thick, leather straps.

She glanced around. The concrete walls looked old and crumbling in places. They appeared to have been painted over many times with the current color resembling the puke-green of a psychiatric ward. In the far right corner, she saw something that resembled a dental chair. In the left corner, a pair of shackles hung from the ceiling.

Where in the world was she? Megan thought.

A door at the far end of the room creaked open and a lady dressed in a nurse's uniform and a man with a very defined limp entered. She recognized the woman as the one who had attacked her and the other two girls back in the dungeon. "Well, hello there, dear," the woman said as she approached the table. "It's about time you woke up. You've been out cold for a few hours. They must have given you a bit too much chloroform."

"Who are you?" Megan asked in a voice that sounded meek to her ears.

"Oh, don't worry about who I am right now, dear. You'll figure that out in due time."

The man stepped around the woman and Megan saw his face clearly for the first time. It resembled a half-melted candle with both eyes drooping from their sockets like paddle balls hanging from their strings. He barely had a nose to speak of and his drooping skin hung around the corners of his mouth in such a way that it looked as if he was constantly smirking. He raised two long, bony hands and tightened the girl's restraints.

"Ouch," said Megan, "that's too tight!"

"Shut your trap, missy, or they will get even tighter," the man with the melted face warned.

Megan did the opposite. In her panic, she let slip a string of inquiries. "Who are you? What are you going to do to me? Where am I?"

"Shut up, you whore!" the man shouted. "No one can hear you, so save your voice."

"Now, Doctor, you need to calm down. We aren't supposed to scare them right away," said the woman.

"I'm just putting a bit of fear in her, Madame. Just enough so that it festers. You know, for later?"

The Doctor and the Madame exchanged a look and then both burst into laughter. The Madame turned back to Megan. "Now, now, dear. Don't you worry. The fun is just beginning."

Megan didn't know what was going on but she had a feeling that whatever they meant by fun was going to be at her expense.

Summer woke in a dark room. She wasn't sure where she was but she wished someone would turn on a light. She hated the dark. It gave her nightmares.

"Hello?" she called. Her voice, weak from hours of inactivity, barely registered a sound. She tried to move but found that her wrists and ankles were firmly bound.

She was freezing and the back of her head throbbed dully. She realized she was lying on something cold but her toes felt like they were on fire.

What the hell?

A door screeched open and the beam of a flashlight penetrated the room. Summer used the opportunity to examine her feet. She saw a string tied to each of her big toes. Attached to the strings was some type of device that resembled a EKG machine. She remembered what those looked like from a hospital show she watched once on television.

The flashlight bobbed about, and Summer heard a woman's voice. "Hello darling, how do you like the dark?"

"You bitch!" Summer screamed. "Who are you? Get me out of here!"

"Well, aren't you a feisty one," the woman said, amused.

"We're going to have fun with this one," a male voice spoke up from somewhere behind the woman. Summer's eyes darted from the dark outline of the woman to a man who looked to be dressed in scrubs; there was something wrong with his face, but she couldn't make out what exactly in the flashlight's dim glow. The woman handed him the flashlight and he shined it first on the EKG machines and then into Summer's eyes, causing her to squeeze them shut for fear of going blind.

"Now, lassie. If you move your feet, you will feel an electric shock. The more you move the higher the voltage will go. So, I suggest you lie still."

"Who the fuck are you?" Summer demanded. "Where am I? You know, my boyfriend is probably looking for me as we speak."

"Shut up, you stupid whore!" The woman smacked her across the face and then got down low so that she could look her directly in the eyes. Summer recognized her as the redhead who had attacked her earlier. "You make another sound and I'll turn the electricity up as high as it will go."

"I'm not afraid of you, you old hag," declared Summer.

"Well, you better be, dear, because this old hag is about to become your worst nightmare."

Who did these people think they were? Kidnapping her, throwing her into the back of a van, and then binding her to a cold table with rope that would electrocute her if she moved? This whole situation was nuts. She had to get out of here.

The man and woman left as abruptly as they had entered, shutting the door behind them. Summer once more found herself in complete darkness. She dared not move because she wasn't sure if the machine would actually electrocute her or if the man had just been bluffing. She had no reason to doubt his word and she really didn't want to find out, so she kept still.

A light appeared from seemingly nowhere. It was pale, barely there, but it was bright enough that Summer was able to make out her surroundings. Her eyes darted around the room. She saw the walls were made of concrete blocks and noticed that the paint was peeling in places. In one of the corners she saw a human-sized metal box. It was from here that the light seemed to emanate. As she watched, a shadowy figure seemed to form out of thin air. It had the shape of a person, but Summer couldn't make out more than that.

Summer closed her eyes and willed it to go away. Whatever that thing was, it scared the hell out of her. When she opened her eyes again she saw it inches from her face as if studying her. Summer screamed.

Chapter 3

When Abby came to, she found herself shackled to metal chains hanging from the ceiling. She tried to pull free but only succeeded in making a lot of noise.

The room was dimly lit. It seemed like only one of the lights above her worked. Then she realized there was only one light, which was right in the center of the ceiling. Her shoes were gone and there was a box under her feet, barely tall enough for her toes to touch.

She had a cloth tied around the lower part of her face with the end of it stuffed in her mouth. Terror clawed at the corners of her mind. Her eyes darted around the room. Opposite her, she saw a metal table. It looked like the ones in funeral homes that they drained dead people on. To the left of it sat a large metal box. The front of it contained a small door just big enough for a fairly small person to fit through.

The room's door opened and a man dressed in scrubs walked in with a pronounced limp and one of the ugliest faces she had ever seen. A woman in a nurse's uniform walked in beside him. Abby, seeing the door open, tried to scream for help, but the cloth muffled her voice almost entirely.

"There, there my darling," the woman crooned. "Calm down. No one can hear you down here. We're underground, you see? Screaming will do you no good. Now, be a good little girl. You will be fine. For now, at least."

The man walked up to her and caressed her stomach, smiling at her creepily. His face looked like it was slipping off his skull. "Now, my pretty. You just stay right here. We'll be back soon."

As they walked out of the room, the man looked over his shoulder and made one of the scariest grins she had ever seen. She wanted to go home. She felt tears rolling down her cheeks and she couldn't breathe. If only there was a way to get this cloth out of her mouth.

Summer woke from a fitful sleep. She must have drifted off; she was very groggy and her mouth felt like sandpaper. The room she was in remained dark, but she could make out a minute bar of light coming from underneath the door. It seemed like she'd been in this place for days. She felt exhausted and stiff from trying to lay still for so long.

She heard the door creak open and strained her face in that direction. "Hello?" she called. "Please, whoever's there, help me!"

"Oh, hello darling," a familiar voice answered. "How are we feeling today? A little less disrespectful, I hope."

"Go to hell!" Summer continued with her fearless act.

The Madame entered with the Doctor trailing behind her. She flipped on a light and Summer saw that they both were carrying buckets, but she couldn't see what was inside. They sat them on the floor, then approached the table.

"Oh, that was the wrong thing to say," said the Doctor. He fiddled with a knob on the machine and Summer felt horrible pain shoot through her toes and up her body so quickly she hardly had time to process what was happening. No sooner had it started then it stopped.

"Now," said the Doctor, "continue to be disrespectful and that's what will keep happening."

The Madame said, "You will address me by saying 'Yes, Madame' or 'Sounds delightful, Madame.' Are we clear?" Summer was pretty sure nothing in this room would ever be 'delightful.' She wondered if she would ever experience such a feeling again? The Madame slammed her hand on the table, startling her. "I said are we clear?"

"Yes, Madame," Summer replied. No need to upset these crazy people any more than necessary. The lights were on so Summer noticed a few things in the room she hadn't been able to see the other day. For one thing, there was what looked like a fireplace set deep in one of the walls with a fire poker propped up next to it. A claw foot bathtub sat along one of the other walls. She also got a good look at the human-sized metal box from which the mysterious light had emanated.

She'd seen something like it in one of those horror movies she and her boyfriend watched on Saturday nights. What was it called again? An iron maiden? Yeah, that sounded right.

"Today is your first punishment, dear," said the Madame. "Now, I'm going to untie you, but if you try to get away, you'll be sorry." She pointed to the bathtub against the wall. "Go ahead and strip down to your undergarments and get into that tub over there."

Summer was hesitant but knew she needed to do what this crazy woman said or she would be in for some serious shit. Yeah, like she wasn't already, but no need to make it any worse. While she was getting undressed, the Madame turned on the bathtub's faucet while the Doctor emptied both buckets into the water. Summer saw that the buckets contained ice. She hoped it was because the water was hot, and the ice would cool it off, but she seriously doubted it.

She walked over to the tub and stared nervously at the ice, which hadn't so much as melted in the water. She was reluctant to get in, but she took a deep breath and did as she was told.

Jesus Christ, I'm being frozen alive! she thought as she felt the biting cold of the icy water. She stood there for what felt like an eternity, hoping her body would get used to the freezing temperature.

"Get in there and sit down!" the Madame yelled.

Summer did as she was told, but hesitantly. Her body shivered uncontrollably. She looked up and saw the Madame and the Doctor towering over her. The Doctor had a knife and the Madame wore a bizarre smile on her face; it kind of reminded Summer of the Joker from those Batman comics.

The Doctor reached down with the knife and cut her bra straps, first one, then the other, then the back. Her bra fell into the cold, icy water. "Oh, dear, are you already cold?" he tittered. "You're going to be in there for a while, so you better figure out how to control that shivering."

Summer felt the knife slide down her back towards her buttocks, just lightly touching her skin. Then it reversed direction and came up between her shoulders and then down her front towards her breasts. She looked down at the knife. It had a sharp tip, but it looked very old and had to be dull because it didn't cut her as it slid across her skin. The doctor moved it in between her breasts and poked her right one with the knife's sharp tip. Summer whimpered.

"Oh, shut up, you whiny whore." The Doctor slipped the knife back between her breasts and poked the left one with the tip. Summer whimpered again, she couldn't help herself. The Doctor moved the knife down her stomach and between her legs and back up to her stomach. Summer knew her look of terror was making the Doctor and this crazy lady insanely happy. It was clear as day on both their faces.

The Doctor slid the blade roughly across her stomach. Summer felt it cut into her flesh and saw blood appear in the water. It wasn't much, but it was enough to send her into a panic. The Doctor moved the knife back up towards her breasts. He then took her right breast in his hand and fondled it, rubbing his thumb over her erect nipple.

He shifted the knife in his other hand and sliced into the top of her breast, deep enough that she thought she might need stitches. Summer screamed. The Doctor did the same thing to her left breast and she blacked out.

Abby's arms were numb from having hung in the shackles for so long. Her lips were dry and cracked from the cloth tied around her mouth. She felt like she had been hanging for hours and she really wanted to sleep. She tried to look around at her surroundings, but couldn't move her head more than an inch in either direction.

The door flew open and in walked the Madame and her Doctor/lackey. "Good day, Red," the Madame said. "Aren't you feeling just splendid this morning?"

The false pleasantness vanished as she looked the room over. Abby saw her tense, as if expecting to see someone or something lurking in the shadows. Her eyes rested on a weird human-sized box that looked like one of those old torture contraptions she saw in a museum once. What was it called again? She couldn't remember but did it really matter? The important thing was what these psychos planned to do with her.

"Now, listen here, Red. It's okay if I call you Red, isn't it? You will only address me by saying 'Yes, Madame' or 'Sounds delightful, Madame.' Do you understand?"

"Yeth, Mahame," she responded, or rather that was the best she could manage due to the cloth in her mouth.

The Madame rewarded her obedience with a stern smile. "Good Subject, I see you catch on quickly."

Good subject, Abby thought. Who is this joker anyway?

The Doctor ran his hands up and down her torso and across her stomach. She twisted in the shackles in a futile attempt to avoid his touch. That just made things worse. Every time she moved, he tightened his grip, sometimes digging his nails into her flesh until she stopped.

The Madame's stern smile tightened. "So, darling, what we have planned for you today is just a small punishment. Just enough to prepare you for the more serious ones ahead. Doesn't that sound delightful?"

The Doctor loosened the cloth around her mouth. Abby tried to talk, but her mouth was so dry that all that came out was a gasp. She really wished these people would give her some water.

The Doctor slapped her across the face. "Don't you even think about speaking back to me! Do you hear me, whore?"

Abby was stunned into silence. She could only watch as the Doctor walked over to a metal table and opened one of its drawers. He turned to her and held up a long, gleaming knife. Abby didn't like this one bit.

He walked over to her, his twisted lips playing at a smile. A strand of drool glistened on his gnarled chin. She didn't notice, her attention was focused entirely on the knife.

The blade was long, at least twelve inches. It looked like something used in a butcher shop to cut through thick layers of meat. He reached towards her with the knife's pointed end. She flinched, which only made his smile broaden. At least, she thought it did. It was hard to tell with that melted face of his. The Doctor steadied her with one hand and then cut the straps of her blouse. He had her shirt off in no time and began next on her pants. Abby couldn't move an inch for fear of being cut. She let out a small whimper and tried not to cry, but a tear rolled down her face despite her best efforts.

"Now, dear, crying is for infants," said the Madame. "If you cry, your punishment will just get worse. So, there's no crying here. Got it?"

Torture? Abby thought. "Yes Madame," she said submissively. Now the Doctor was between her legs. Oh God, what was going to happen to her? What type of "punishment" was she expected not to cry about? Her shirt and pants were off now and she just hung there in nothing more than her bra and underwear.

The Madame walked behind her and pulled something off the wall. She then stepped over to Abby's left side. "See this, darling?" She held up a coiled length of cord. "It's a whip. I told you that you shouldn't have tried to scream. You get five lashes. Doctor, will you do the honor?"

"With pleasure," the Doctor tittered.

What the hell? Abby thought.

CRACK!

One lash right across the chest. The pain was intense, like nothing she had ever felt before. Her mouth was so dry she couldn't manage a proper scream. All that came out was

a squeak, high and ragged. It was the best she could do.

"Do you like it?"

CRACK!

Jesus! She thought wildly. *There are people who actually like this?*

CRACK!

"Red!" the Madame shrieked. "I can't hear you! I said do you like it? Would you like another?"

Abby knew that if she said no, she would just get more, so she said, "Yes, Madame, please may I have another?"

"But of course." The Doctor was behind her now, drawing back the lash even as he spoke.

CRACK!

Oh shit! thought Abby. She didn't know which felt worse; being hit on her front or her back.

CRACK!

She managed a pathetic "Ahhhhhhhh" and then fell silent. Thank God that was it. She didn't think she could take another lash. Already she could feel welts forming on her chest and back. She prayed they were done with her. If this was a little taste of things to come, she couldn't fathom what worse things they had in store for her.

Just when she thought they had finished, the Doctor sliced into one of her throbbing welts. Abby drew her mouth wide in a silent scream. She felt him stick a finger inside her wound and begin digging around. She didn't know if hell was real, but if so, this must be it. Through the tears in her eyes she saw Madame hand him something. "Don't worry, Red, we're only implanting a tracking device. We can't have you trying to escape, now can we?"

No, Abby thought. Can't have your "subjects" ruining all your fun, now can we?

After they inserted the device in her back, she felt the Doctor sew her up like some life-size rag doll. Her legs felt damp. She must have wet herself, which made her feel absurdly embarrassed. Abby never knew that pain could drain so much out of you. Then again, she had never experienced pain as bad as this. God, how she wanted to cry.

"Now, Red, be still. We're just going to put this salve on your wounds so that they heal faster. We need you good and infection free for next time. Oh, you peed on yourself. Well, there's nothing doing, you'll have to lay in it. Maybe that'll teach you to keep yourself under control next time."

Next time? thought Abby. She wasn't sure how many more "next times" she could take.

"Once we're done here," the Madame said, "we'll untie you so you can try to move around the room. You need to stay in good health. The door is locked from the outside, so don't even try to escape. We'll know if you so much as touch that doorknob."

Next time. The words danced crazily in her head. She didn't know what she'd done to end up here but she was sure she didn't deserve this kind of treatment. Nobody did.

The Madame untied her and helped her stand. She was glad she was out of the shackles, but her arms felt like limp noodles and her legs could hardly hold her weight.

"Pleasant dreams, dear." The Madame and her little toad of a Doctor exited the room without bothering to shut off the light. Abby heard a lock click and knew she was locked inside. She sat down on the cold concrete floor and took in her surroundings. The room was filled with shadows; they engulfed the walls, the floor, the ceiling. One in particular stood out because it looked as if it was crawling towards her on all fours. That was crazy, though. But no crazier than anything else in this loony bin.

God, she was in hell.

Abby scooted backwards across the floor, trying to give herself as much space as she could from that creepy shadow. It passed her by, though, and continued around the room. Abby followed it with her eyes, fascinated despite her fear and pain. The shadow stopped next to a large drain in the floor and just hovered there as if trying to get Abby's attention.

The shadow terrified her, but maybe it was also trying to tell her something. Abby closed her eyes and wished for it to go away. She wished for a lot of things over the course of that long night. None of them came true.

Chapter 4

SMACK!

Megan woke with a start. The Madame and Doctor hovered over her, smiling like a couple of dolts. "Why, hello there, dear. How are we feeling today?" the Madame crooned. Megan began to cry. She wanted out of this place. She wanted to go home. Most of all, she wanted these sick fucks to go to hell.

"Oh, my darling, it's not time to cry yet. Today is the day we start your punishments. Aren't you excited about that?"

Megan had no idea what the Madame was talking about, but knew for a fact that she wanted nothing to do with whatever weird games they had planned.

The lady started to undo the restraints on Megan's wrists. "Now dear, if you try to escape once I take these off, you will endure even worse punishments. I guarantee you do not want that. Do you hear?"

"Okay," said Megan.

"Listen, you little shit, you will never address me with anything but 'Yes, Madame' or 'sounds delightful, Madame.' Do you understand?"

"Yes, Madame," Megan responded with her head down. If she had to look at either of them she might burst into tears again and she didn't want to give them the satisfaction.

"That's a good little mouse, you catch on quick." Madame untied the rest of Megan's restraints. She even helped her to her feet and guided her to a chair in the room's corner.

It looks like a dentist chair, Megan thought. Whatever was about to happen, Megan was pretty sure she wasn't going to like it. Madame instructed her to sit in the chair.

"Yes, Madame," Megan said. She was completely terrified, but something told her that if she showed even the slightest hint of fear, her situation would only worsen.

"Now, dear, what we are going to do today is a little bit of a practice punishment to get you ready for the real thing."

Oh God, Megan thought. "Yes, Madame."

"Very good. Now we're going to put the chair back a bit so that your head is lower than the rest of your body. Then we're going to start the drip."

Madame tied the restraints around her chest and her legs. Then she pushed a button on the chair's side and it began to lean back. Next thing Megan knew, she was staring at the ceiling and the top of the wall behind her. On the ceiling, she saw a nozzle that looked kind of like a sprinkler. Water dripped from it directly onto her forehead. This process repeated itself again and again.

Chinese water torture? Megan thought. *You've got to be kidding me.*

Megan heard something clinking in front of her. She couldn't see what it was from her prone position, but she had an inkling that it wasn't good. Madame bent over and whispered in her ear. "I'm just going to put this ball gag in your mouth so you can't scream."

"Yes, Madame," Megan said, shocked.

Madame put the ball gag in Megan's mouth. The gag was very uncomfortable, and Megan found that she couldn't move her mouth at all, let alone scream if she had to.

"We're going to start your punishments with a cut to your arm. Not to worry, though, we know you're a lefty, so we'll start with the right one first."

Megan's eyes widened at the thought. She attempted a "Yes, Madame," but, with the gag in her mouth, that wasn't going to happen.

"I'll just assume you're okay with your treatments because, well, you have to be or things will get much worse for you," Madame said. "We just feel that it's important to warn you what we're about to do. It feeds your fear, and your fear feeds us, you see. Isn't it wonderful how we benefit each other?"

Megan felt pain bloom along the upper part of her right arm. She cried out, but the gag muffled the sound. There was no one to hear her anyway. She had been cut with some sort of sharp object. "Wasn't that just delightful darling?" Madame crooned. Megan shook her head. Madame frowned. "You'll appreciate the painful distraction soon enough, you'll see."

Water continued to drip on Megan's head. Her arm began to throb. She felt a stabbing sensation, like someone was digging inside her wound. She felt tears running down her face and was thankful these crazy ass people couldn't hear her scream. Seriously, what was wrong with them?

"In case you're wondering what we're doing, the Doctor is placing a tracking device inside you so that we can keep track of all your movements. This way, we always know where you are." The Madame grabbed a needle and thread from a kit she had brought with her and deftly stitched up the slit in Megan's arm. Megan tried to jerk away, but the Doctor held down her arm. She laid still, but felt fresh tears running down her face.

"You'll need to go to the infirmary every day to make sure this doesn't get infected," the Doctor said. "We can't have you dying on us this early in the game, can we?"

Megan didn't know why she was here or what she had done, but she had a sinking feeling that things were just going to get worse. After all, that's what Madame had said, right? Today was just a bit of practice to get her ready for the real thing.

Madame untied her and helped her off the chair and back to the table. Once she had her laid out flat, she tied her up again. "Now, dearie, don't you try to get away. This door will be locked from the outside. That way, we don't have to worry about you leaving us unexpectedly."

Megan stared at their backs as they left the room. After she heard the door shut and lock behind them, she glanced at the wall to her left and saw what looked like a shadowy figure. At first she thought it might be her own shadow, but that couldn't be. This shadow was on all fours. She didn't know what to think about that, but it scared her all the same.

Megan was in and out of consciousness. She opened her eyes, looked around, and didn't see the Doctor or Madame. Her arm was numb and throbbing. She was tired of being tied up and she wanted off this cold table. She knew those terrible people would be back to do awful things to her.

She tried to sit up but didn't get very far. She felt dizzy, but that subsided quickly. Voices sounded outside the door. A moment later, the Madame walked in with the Doctor in tow. They approached the table and stared down at Megan. "Let's get you to the infirmary, dear," the Madame said. "Don't want an infection to kick in now do we?" They untied her and walked out of the room without another word.

Megan followed the two down the dark, mildew-scented hallway . After walking a few feet, she looked to her right and saw a really nice room that didn't belong in this horrible place. It had a plush, comfortable looking couch, soft-looking white carpet, and emerald-painted walls.

Next to it was another room with white walls, a white bed with white sheets, and white bookshelves. It reminded her of her aunt's house. At the far end of the room there was a black, wrought iron staircase that appeared to go up forever.

The Madame and Doctor took her into the white room and told her to lay on the bed. The Doctor tended to the wound in her arm, then gave her an aspirin, which she took without question despite her better judgement. He then put salve on her cut, wrapped it in gauze, and told her to go into the first room, which he called the "waiting area."

She immediately went to the couch and laid down.In a matter of seconds, she was fast asleep.

Abby laid in the fetal position on the table, her arms bound. Her back hurt like a bitch. She drifted in and out of consciousness. At one point, she woke to see Madame sitting in a chair close by.

"I see you're awake. What say we get you off that table and to the Doctor for treatment?"

Madame untied Abby and helped her up. She led her through the door, down the hall, and to the infirmary where the Doctor awaited her, his utensils gleaming under the sterile operating room lights. He grinned and gestured for her to have a seat.

Summer woke up feeling very weak. She looked around and saw she was in a white room with Madame sitting next to her. She felt something in her left arm and looked down. There was an IV line attached to the crook of her elbow. She saw stitches in both breasts, and her stomach bore stitches as well.

"You've been asleep all day," the Madame said in her usual cheery yet creepy tone. "We need you up and walking around so we put a chip in you to keep you from escaping." Summer began to speak but the Madame held up a finger for silence. "Yes, I know, how utterly thoughtful of us, right?"

"Yes, Madame."

"Come, dear, up you go." Madame slipped her hands under Summer's arms and helped her to her feet. The movement hurt Summer's stomach, but she didn't want to cry for fear of having something else insane done to her.

Madame and the Doctor helped Summer down the hallway to the infirmary. Summer stumbled even with the two holding onto her. It was as if her legs were made of rubber. The hallway was freezing, and the linoleum floor felt like ice under her bare feet. The whole place smelled of mildew.

A few feet down the hallway, Summer saw a bright room filled with furniture. A familiar looking girl sat on a couch, talking with another girl in an egg chair with blue lining. She thought they were the ones she'd met earlier but couldn't remember their names. One thing she did know: they needed to work together if they were going to get out of this hellhole.

Summer's captors carried her past the room containing the two girls to one decked out completely in white. It had a large glass window and Summer stretched her neck, hoping for a glimpse of the building's exterior, but all she saw was the brick wall of the adjoining wing. Madame and the Doctor sat her on the bed. The Doctor put salve on all her wounds, wrapped them with gauze, gave her a pill that she at first refused but was made to swallow under threat of pain, and some crutches to help her get around on her own.

Madame told her to go into the waiting room, which Summer assumed was the room that they had passed when coming here. She used the crutches awkwardly at first, but after a little trial and error she made her way to the waiting room and settled into one of the recliners. Her wounds screamed in protest, but she did her best to ignore them as she turned to the other girls. One was tall and athletic looking, the other had long red hair and a mousy way about her.

"What's going on here?" Summer asked.

"Beats me. We've just been talking about how to get out of here is all," said the athletic girl. "I'm Megan by the way and this is Abigail."

"It's just Abby," the redhead said. "And we've already met."

Megan scoffed. "Well, excuse me."

Abby smiled shyly at Summer. "Only grownups call me Abigail. And three heads are definitely better than two, especially if one of them is as dense as Megan's. What say we work together?"

Before Summer could answer, the three of them heard the Madame's pleasantly cruel voice:

"Yoo-hoo! Girls! It's dinnertime!"

They looked at each other skeptically, but got up just the same. Really, what choice did they have? Madame appeared in the waiting room's doorway and led them through a long, empty hallway to a luxurious looking dining room. Its floor was an immaculate white and black marble; a huge chandelier hung from the ceiling fifteen feet over a long, polished table overflowing with every kind of food imaginable.

The girls gawked at the table. There were hamburgers with all the fixings, mashed potatoes, sweet potatoes, tacos, ham, turkey, three kinds of salad, caviar, filet mignon, portabella mushrooms, crab legs and lobster with butter to dip it in, tons of different kinds of shrimp and shellfish. Not to mention all the desserts! Cheesecakes, pies, Jell-O, sweet bread, you name it, it was on the table.

The Madame smacked her hands together. "Okay, girls, enough staring. Dig in! You all must be famished."

"But, we can't possibly . . ." Megan began.

"What? Eat all of it?" The Madame's dark eyes glinted in the room's dim lighting. "Oh, don't worry your pretty little heads about that. Just eat until you can't possibly eat anymore, then I'll show you to your rooms."

The Madame shut the dining room doors behind her as she left.

Our rooms? thought Summer. What kind of place is this anyway?

The girls were starving but also suspicious.

"Should we?" Abby asked.

"What if it's poisoned?" Megan said.

"Well, at least we'll die with a full stomach," Summer reasoned.

None of them could argue with that. They threw their cares aside and set to gorging themselves on the delectable meal set out before them.

They all felt like they hadn't eaten in days. None of them talked much because they were too busy stuffing their mouths. After they had gobbled their fill the Madame appeared and escorted them back to the sitting room by the stairs.

"Now you can each run along and pick whatever room you like. Choose carefully because it will be the place where you spend the most time during these next seven days of healing. There is a phone in every room. You can't call out with it but if you get hungry, all you have to do is call down to the kitchen and order whatever your little heart's desire. Go now, and do try to have fun."

Chapter 5

The girls walked up the winding iron staircase. At the top, they saw a long hallway with doors on either side. They had no idea how many doors there were, but they seemed to stretch on forever. The girls started with the first door and made their way down the hallway.

The first room had a trampoline right in the middle of it. Abby was ecstatic. It wasn't as big as the one she had at home, but she was happy to have one here to bounce her cares away on. The ceilings were so high that she could jump as long and as hard as she wanted without fear of bumping her head. This first room was going to be Abby's no doubt about it.

The three of them decided to meet here after they finished looking at the other rooms. There were quite a few left to explore and they picked the ones that best catered to their extracurricular interests. It was almost like each room was chosen after a thorough study of their lives. All three of them were uncomfortable with this concept, but knew that they needed to do what Madame said if they didn't want to be punished.

Megan picked a room with a mini water park in it. She had no idea how they supplied the water for the slides, but they were there and she fell in love with them at first glance. The room had two slides, both very curvy, with a small pool situated at the far end. There was also a lazy river around the whole length of the room that connected with the pool.

Summer picked a room that contained every video game system one could desire. Murals of all her favorite X-Men decorated the walls. She wished she could've stayed in that room all day, sampling every game on every system. The TV was a massive thing, taking up nearly one whole section of wall. Summer picked up the TV's remote and pushed the power button. A concert appeared on the giant screen. She saw with both delight and wonder that it featured one of her favorite bands.

After playing with the remote for a while, she realized that at the touch of a button, she could view a concert for whatever band she wanted. Summer didn't even have to tell it which band to play. Somehow it just knew. She decided to play some Depeche Mode. A massive image of Dave Gahan singing about how words were so very unnecessary popped on the screen. Despite her pain, Summer couldn't help but smile. If she was in hell, she figured she could do a lot worse than this.

As agreed, they met back in Abby's room later that night. Their discussion centered on a plan of escape, but they hid the details behind talks of boys and school; things they figured their captors would expect girls their age to talk about. Megan had suggested that their rooms might be bugged. Summer didn't think it was that far-fetched a notion. If the Madame could create enormous rooms filled with the girls' wildest imaginings, then eavesdropping on them should be a breeze by comparison.

The three of them sat on Abby's king-size bed (they all had the same one, complete with four soft organic pillows and a white Siberian down comforter).

"Did either of you see a shadow when you were in the dungeons?" Summer asked.

"What do you mean 'shadow'?" Abby hugged one of the pillows against her and rocked slowly back and forth.

"I mean, like a living shadow. It moves around, almost like—"

"A ghost!" Megan cut it.

"Yeah!" Summer and Abby shouted at the same time. Abby clamped her hand over her mouth and looked at her companions with wide, frightened eyes. Summer scanned the room and then giggled. She motioned for the others to do the same.

"No way would Steve Rawlings date your skanky ass," Summer proclaimed loudly. In a lower voice she said, "I saw it crawling on all fours. It stayed in this one corner of the room, like it was trying to tell me something."

"Who's Steve Rawlings?" Megan whispered. Summer slapped her knee and Megan

caught on. "Oh, uh, I wouldn't want to date him anyway! Probably one of those weird goth guys, right?" She threw a wink at Summer, who simply rolled her eyes.

"It gave me the creeps," Abby said into her pillow.

"Oh my god! That's the way I felt too!" exclaimed Megan.

"What if it was a ghost?" Summer asked. "I mean, seriously, is that stranger than anything else we've seen around here?"

Abby buried her face deeper into her pillow. "What does it want?"

"I don't know," Summer said, "but I don't think it's dangerous. Not like that bitch and her manservant."

"The Incredible Melting Man," Megan said and this time their giggling was genuine.

"I got that same feeling," Abby said to Summer. "You know, about the ghost-shadow. Like it was trying to help us."

"Maybe we should let it," Summer said.

Megan scoffed. "What is it with you goth types? The first creepy thing to come slithering along and you're all like: 'Oh, let's make it our friend!' I mean, seriously!"

Summer looked from Megan to Abby, her expression serious. "I didn't say we should make it our friend. I'm suggesting that we use it to help get us out of here."

"Yeah? And how're we going to do that?" Megan asked.

"I don't know," Summer said. "That's what we're here to talk about, right?"

She gestured for the two to come closer. The girls huddled together and for the rest of the night all potential avenues of escape were mulled over and ultimately dismissed as either impossible or too risky to try. They agreed that the shadow-ghost helping them was a long shot, but they would try to contact it should the thing appear again.

In the absence of any more ideas they settled into the solace of each other's arms and tried to forget the horrors they had endured these last few days, as well as the horrors yet to come.

The girls hung out together for the next few days. They played video games, jumped on the trampoline (except for Summer, who had the most recovering to do physically), and fully enjoyed the waterpark. They became close very quickly as only people trapped in such horrendous situations can.

They played music all day and slept in the empyrean beds with down comforters and silk sheets at night. It felt like heaven, though they had to remind themselves they were as far from that abode of God as one could get.

Even though there was no mention of torture, they knew it was only a matter of time before it started again. That is, if they failed to escape from here—wherever here was. They thought they might be in an old mental hospital, but the place was unlike any hospital they had ever heard of. There were the enormous rooms that could accommodate themed waterparks for one thing, and the ghostly shadow for another.

It was a very strange time for the girls. They didn't know why they had been brought here or what their captors ultimately had in store for them. They couldn't even remember when they had been kidnapped. Everything seemed muddled, like a sort of fever dream. All the girls knew for sure was that they had to get as far from this place as they could.

Unfortunately, the time spent healing in their luxuriant rooms with every convenience literally at the push of a button had dulled their urgency to escape. The need to do so was still there, just assigned a less significant role in their daily activities. In her more lucid moments,

Summer wondered if they had been drugged by the Madame, or if maybe the place itself was alive and was somehow draining them of their will to escape.

The Madame allowed them to wander wherever they liked. Abby was hesitant to leave the comforts of their rooms, but Summer and Megan understood that the key to their freedom was not water slides and trampolines but the grimy depths of the hospital's lower levels; what the Madame called "The Devil's Dungeon." Like the rest of the place, the dungeon was enormous, almost like an underground castle. The hallways were maze-like, and the girls had gotten themselves lost on a couple of occasions, but they always ended up where they started, as if they were walking in circles.

They searched for the ghostly shadow but saw no sign of it. They contemplated the drains in the floors but didn't see how they could fit through them. Any door they entered led either to one of the torture rooms (always a wake-up call that they needed to get the hell out of here) or another hallway.

After a week of this, the Madame brought all three girls to the examination room where the Doctor announced that their wounds were healing nicely.

"Fantastic!" the Madame said. "We shall resume the punishments at once."

The girls, anticipating this inevitability, decided their best option would be to fight their captors. None of them had seen the brute that brought them here. Maybe he was out cruising the neighborhoods in his white van, seeking more girls for the dungeon. At any rate, if it was just the Madame and her manservant then they thought they might stand a chance. There were three of them, after all. Megan, being the most athletic, said she would lead the charge when the time came. Summer and Abby were happy to let her.

This wasn't Madame's first rodeo, however. That night, she mixed sleeping medication with their food. All three were out cold before the Doctor, playing the part of butler, served dessert.

Abby, Summer, and Megan woke on the floor of one of the dungeon's torture rooms. All three had ball gags in their mouths. Their arms were tied behind their backs. Abby recognized it as the room her first round of torturing had taken place in because there was an iron maiden in the far corner.

They looked at each other and the fear in their eyes conveyed a mutual thought: *Oh no, not again!*

The door opened and the Madame and Doctor sauntered in. The Doctor carried scissors on a silver tray that glittered in the overhead fluorescent lighting. "You young ladies wound us." The Doctor sat down the tray and raised the long, serrated scissors as if displaying a conqueror's sword. "We give you your heart's desire. We feed you, care for you, and you repay our kindness by plotting to escape?"

The girls shook their heads fervently.

"Liars," the Madame cooed.

The Doctor loomed over Abby, stroking her hair with his free hand . "No use denying it. We know your type. Always ungrateful. Always unsatisfied. Others sacrifice for you. They work their fingers to the bone for you. Yet you always want more." He snatched a fistful of hair and cut it free with the scissors. Abby tried to scream but the ball gag muffled her cries. The Doctor dangled the lock of red curls in front of her. "You have such beautiful hair, girl. I bet it took you years to grow it so long and lustrous. The thought of losing it must be unbearable."

Tears stood out in Abby's eyes. The Madame saw this and scoffed. "Oh, darling, are you mad because we cut your hair? Well, get over it! That's the least of your problems, so quit it with the crying."

The Doctor cut Summer and Megan's hair in the same manner. He then removed the ball gags and untied their arms. The girls remained knelt, not sure if they were finished but daring to hope that the worst might be over. Maybe this was more of a psychological type of torture than a physical one, Summer thought. Maybe their captors were just reminding them who was the boss.

However, their hopes were dashed when the Madame handed Abby and Megan some of Summer's hair and Summer some of Abby and Megan's. "Now girls, we are going to leave you all here. When we return, we expect you to have eaten every strand of that hair in your hands. If you haven't, well, we'll just have to wash it down your throats with something warm and bitter. Understood?"

"Yes, Madame," the girls said dismally.

The Doctor and Madame left the girls to their task. Abby and Megan began to cry. However, they stopped at Summer's urging. Crying wouldn't help, and they had more important things to consider, like how exactly they were supposed to eat a handful of hair without choking on it. "Shouldn't be that hard," Abby said. "My cat always seems to be coughing up hairballs and she's just fine."

"We're not eating hair," Summer said.

"Damn straight," Megan said. "But how do we get rid of it?"

They looked around and spotted a grate on the floor near the iron maiden. Abby figured it was designed to catch the blood such a device would sap from its victims. The thought of being trapped inside that spike-covered cabinet sent chills down her back. She wasn't as strong as her two companions. If not for them she would've likely gone mad the first day here. But even with their strength lending her courage, she wasn't sure how much more of this craziness she could take.

The three of them tiptoed to the rectangle-shaped grate and knelt around it. The thing was large but not so large that they felt they could squeeze through it to the sewers below. At least, not without a little help. Megan, whose father worked in construction and had shown her a few tricks of the trade, suggested that she might be able to widen it a little given time and the right tools. "The concrete's old and crumbling," she said. "See how it's already deteriorating in places? I bet a strong piece of metal would be enough to chip it away."

"It's worth a shot," Summer agreed. "That is, if we can remember where this room is. This dungeon's a maze and there's so many rooms. We might not find this one again."

"We could leave a trail," Abby suggested.

Megan shrugged. "Sounds good, but how?"

"Maybe . . ." Abby considered a moment. "Maybe we can cut the palms of our hands. On our way back to our rooms we smear our blood on sections of the walls. Just enough at each turn in the hallway that it'll create a trail we can follow."

"Not a bad idea," Summer said. "Come on, help me move this grate before those whackos come back."

They slipped their slender fingers through the cast iron lattice and pulled until the grate popped out of the floor. "Okay, good. We've got to move quickly. Here, hand me the hair." Summer took the tufts of hair and stuffed them all down the hole in the floor. They made sure every strand was gone before they slid the grate back in place and resumed their positions on the floor.

"Hey, I just thought of something," Megan said. "How're we supposed to cut our hands?"

"I saw a nail in the wall near the door," Summer said. "Maybe one of us can use it on our way out while the others distract that bitch and her boyfriend."

"Yeah, but, you know, rusty old nails might give us tetanus," Abby pointed out.

Megan rolled her eyes. "I'd take lockjaw over whatever these sickos have in store for us any day."

"It's okay, Abby." Summer offered a thin smile. "You can act as the distraction then."

Abby's face went pale but, to her credit, she didn't protest. They had no idea how much time had passed, but it wasn't long before the

Doctor and Madame returned. "How did it taste, girls?" asked the Doctor with a slanted snarl that they assumed passed for a smile.

"Get some sleep," the Madame said. "You'll need it for what we have in store for you."

The girls rose. Summer looked to Abby who returned her look like a condemned prisoner staring into the face of her executioner. Summer felt pity for her but quickly snuffed it. There was no room for such feelings in a place like this.

Abby let out a groan and fell to the floor, nearly tripping the Doctor, who watched her with detached, clinical wonder. Abby began to drum the heels of her feet against the concrete floor and thrash her arms up and down. She rolled her eyes up into her head, revealing the whites.

"What's this now?" the Madame called.

"She appears to be having an epileptic fit," the Doctor said dispassionately.

"Here now, stop that!" the Madame demanded. "Stop it at once or there will be severe consequences!"

"It's the stress," Summer pleaded. "Please, she needs help, not—"

"Quiet!" The Doctor backhanded Summer before she could finish speaking. She fell on her rump and remained there, watching as Abby's thrashing began to diminish.

"I said stop this. Now." The Madame did not sound at all amused. The thrashing stopped, and Abby moaned and rubbed her forehead. The Madame grabbed her by the arms and pulled her to her feet. "Think that was funny, do you?"

"I don't . . . I don't know what you mean," Abby slurred. "What happened?"

"Oh, nothing yet, dear, but just wait." The Madame clamped her hand around Abby's arm and led her out of the room with the Doctor trailing close behind.

Summer got to her feet and glanced at Megan, who revealed the small gash in the palm of her right hand, where blood had begun to well. She threw Summer a wink as they followed the group out the door.

Chapter 6

That night, the girls made their way into the depths of the Devil's Dungeon. Summer used a candle she confiscated from a chandelier that hung in her room to follow the trail of blood Megan had left earlier that day. "So, you didn't get in trouble at all?" she asked Abby, who crept along behind her, looking like a scared mouse in the dim glow of the candle light.

"No, it was weird," Abby said. "She just told me she was sorely disappointed in me and escorted me to my room."

"That epileptic thing was brilliant," Megan said from where she brought up the rear. She clutched the steel leg from her bed frame in both hands. Her two companions had helped her disassemble it from her bed to use as a digging implement. It was a bitch to get off and would be an even bigger bitch to put back on, but it looked sturdy enough to do the job.

"Not to mention heavy enough to cave in that skank Madame's head," she had boasted. Though now as they trudged along in search of Megan's castoff blood, her assertion sounded less confident to her ears. She continued to look over her shoulder for any sign of their captors. If she did see them odds were good she'd wet herself rather than put up a fight.

"Thanks," Abby said. "It was kinda spur of the moment. I thought for sure Madame was going to take an inch or two off my hide for it."

"Well, we're not out of the woods yet," Summer said. "So keep it down, will you?"

They followed the trail of blood and occasional bloody handprints Megan had left on the stone walls, but all it did was take them in circles.

"I don't understand," Megan said when they came across the same maroon palm print along a corner wall. "We should've come by the door by now. I made sure to mark it."

"It's this place," Summer said. "It doesn't want to let us go."

"Don't start with your goth bullshit," Megan snapped.

"I'm not doing anything of the sort," Summer said. "Don't be so thick-headed, it's obvious some strange shit's going on around here."

Abby pointed past Summer's nose. "What was that?"

Summer raised the candle. In its dim, wavering glow, they made out a shadowy form slinking along the wall several feet ahead of them. The form appeared to be human, but it was hard to tell because every time the girls' eyes grew accustomed to it the form would either change or retreat once more into the darkness.

"That's it!" Abby whispered excitedly. "It's the shadow-ghost!"

"No way," Megan said.

Abby looked at her companion, indignant. "What do you mean 'no way'? It's right there!"

"I think . . . I think it's trying to tell us something," Summer said.

They watched as the shadowy figure traced itself along a section of the wall that had, but a moment before, not existed. All three of them would have sworn to it. Cautiously, they drew closer until the light from Summer's candle revealed a door shut and barred from the outside.

"This is freaking me out," Megan said. "Where the hell did that door come from?"

"I think it's the door we're looking for." Summer drew closer with the light. "Yeah, see, here's Megan's blood!"

Megan stepped closer and examined the maroon palm print she had left behind earlier that day. "Yep, this's the door all right." She looked around for the shadow-ghost, but it was gone as quickly as it appeared. "You know, it'd be really nice if something around here made some sense."

"We're wasting time," Summer said. Here, hold this." She handed the candle to Abby and then, with Megan's help, lifted the heavy bar from the door and set it aside.

Megan nodded to Summer. "After you."

"Gee, thanks." Summer pushed the door open and the three of them entered carefully. Abby handed the candle back to Summer, who used it to confirm the room was clear. Realizing they were alone, all three relaxed a little. Summer had Abby watch the hallway from the door, which they left open a crack so that they could hear anyone approaching.

She and Megan made their way to the grate on the floor.

"Do you really think we can get to the sewers from here?" Megan asked.

"I don't know," Summer admitted. "But it's the only plan we've got."

"What about those tracking things they put in us? Won't they be able to detect us wherever we go?"

Summer slipped her fingers through the lattice and nodded to Megan to do the same. "We'll worry about that later. Now heave."

They lifted the grate from the floor and stared into the drain's blackened depths.

"It stinks," Megan said, pinching her nose.

Summer grinned. "Just think of it as the smell of freedom."

"Freedom couldn't come equipped with an air freshener?" Megan settled on her knees, raised the steel leg, and got to work.

"What are you girls up to?" the Madame asked Abby the following morning.

The two of them stood in the very room the three of them had occupied hours earlier. Megan and Summer weren't here today. The Doctor was taking care of them in another section of the dungeon. It was only Abby and the Madame. Abby, frightened to begin with, nearly wet herself when the Madame began questioning her. Did she know about their plot? And if so, how much had she uncovered?

"What're you talking about?" she managed to say. Her throat felt as if it had constricted to the size of a straw.

The Madame stepped closer. "Don't play games, my dear. You're not very good at it. I know you three are up to something, Madame can always tell. So, let's have it."

Abby resisted the urge to look at the grate only a few feet away. They had spent half the night attempting to widen the drain's hole. They had stopped around four this morning, partly out of exhaustion but mostly out of fear of being caught. They managed to chip away a lot of the age-worn concrete, though. Abby figured that all it would take was one more night and the opening would be wide enough for them all to squeeze through.

Of course, it would all be for nothing if their captors found out what they were up to, so Abby kept her eyes focused on the Madame no matter how much it unnerved her to do so. Her companions were likely also being interrogated by the Doctor. If they could just keep their lips zipped for one more night, they might just make it out of here alive and in one piece.

"I d-don't know what you're t-talking about," she stuttered.

"You know the penalty for lying to me, girl?"

"I'm not lying!"

Abby backed away, but the Madame caught her arm and forced her to look at the iron maiden that sat open in the corner, its interior studded with spikes. Their points gleamed sharply in the overhead light.

"The penalty is that you spend the day in the iron maiden. How would you like that, dear?"

"No!" Abby tried to pull free, but Madame held on tight.

"Oh yes. Contrary to popular belief, the spikes don't pierce your flesh when the box is shut. No, so long as you remain perfectly still there is just enough room to avoid the points. But as the day wears on you will grow tired. You will want to lean against something, to rest." The Madame grinned crookedly. "And that's when the fun begins."

"Please, we're not up to anything!" Abby begged. "We've been good, just like you wanted! Please, you've gotta believe me!"

"Oh, dear, I wish I could, but girls are notorious at keeping secrets. Maybe a few hours in the box will loosen your tongue, yes?"

"No!" Abby screamed. "No, please!"

She managed to slip free of the Madame's grasp, but as she ran for the door the Madame's brawny goon stepped through it and caught her in his large arms. She kicked and screamed but to no avail. The goon silently carried her to the iron maiden as the Madame looked on, still smiling that crooked smile. "Come now, get in. Stop wasting time!"

The goon released her, and Abby stood, staring at the spike-covered interior. She realized she was going in one way or another. If she made them do it, she was liable to cut herself badly on those sharp spikes. With a sigh that ended in a whimper, Abby stepped into the box.

"There now, that's more like it," the Madame crooned. "This will be a time of contemplation. Use it wisely."

Abby turned around, careful to avoid the spikes, and stared out at the Madame and her goon. She hated this. She just wanted to go home. She didn't know what was wrong with these demented people, but she wanted this done and over with. The Madame shut and locked the door. "Try not to stand too stiffly," she said. "It'll only tire you out that much faster."

The Madame turned out the lights as she and the goon left. Abby found herself alone and terrified. The box was incredibly tight. She could feel the points of the spikes poking at her arms and legs. They were gentle pokes now, but how long before she felt them tear through her flesh? How long did she think she could keep this up before exhaustion got the better of her?

Abby began to panic. She knew this was the last thing she should do but couldn't help herself. Tears ran down her cheeks. She wanted to go home. God, how she wanted to go home. She wanted to see her mom and dad. To jump on her trampoline. She wanted to go swimming in the ocean, to gossip with her friends between classes at school. She wanted to be anywhere but here. She was all alone. No way was she going to make it on her own. She might as well come clean and tell the Madame what she wanted to hear. Already she felt her body stiffening. Her panic deepened. There was no way out of here. She was going to die here all alone. There was no way out! No way—

She felt a presence in the box with her. She wasn't sure how, there was barely enough room for her alone, but it was there all the same. She felt the faint whisper of a hand caress her cheek. The touch was cold but soothing. She felt herself start to calm down. She wasn't alone after all.

Was it their shadow-ghost? She couldn't see anything due to the darkness, but somehow, she thought it was. It seemed as if the thing wanted to help them. *Good,* she thought, *let it*. Whatever the thing was, Abby was glad it was on their side, and that it was here now to comfort her. With its help, maybe she would make it through the next few hours.

It felt like an eternity before the Madame returned for Abby. "Oooohhh, hello dear, how are you feeling?" she asked as she opened the iron maiden's door and allowed the fluorescent lighting to flood in. Abby blinked against the brightness. She felt woozy, disoriented. Her body was in tremendous pain.

"Oh, look at that. Looks like you leaned back." The Madame frowned sympathetically. "Here, let me help you out of there and get you to the Doctor."

Abby was too weak to protest. She wanted out of this damned cabinet, sure, but she didn't want to see the Doctor's leering, half-melted face either. More than anything she wanted to go back to her room, curl up on her bed, and sleep for an age or more.

She had tried to stay awake inside the iron maiden but had nodded off a few times and fallen against the spikes. The wounds felt superficial, but they had worked wonders as a deterrent against sleep. She had done her best to remain perfectly still and her back was killing her now as a result. Her legs had turned to jelly long ago and as the Madame led her from the room she thought the floor had all the consistency of her trampoline's vinyl padding. It was all she could do not to fall down.

"We ended up keeping you in there much longer than intended," the Madame went on. "Nearly three days! Believe me, I'm just as shocked as you are! However did you manage to stay upright for so long?"

It was my shadow friend, Abby thought. It stayed by my side the whole time. Or at least Abby thought it had. The thing may have disappeared for short periods of time, maybe to lend comfort to the other girls as it had her. Whatever the reason, she would not have survived three days (Jesus, was it really that long?) without its company.

Abby opened her mouth, intending to spin some elaborate lie—the last thing she wanted was for the Madame to find out about their ghostly helper—but nothing came out. Her throat felt dry as a prune. And she was famished. What she wouldn't give for one of their captors' extravagant feasts right about now.

The Madame feigned concern. "You poor thing, you must be thirsty. Let's get you some water." She snapped her fingers at the burly goon who lingered in the shadows. He nodded and disappeared through a door. The Madame walked Abby to the common room. Abby was relieved to see Summer and Megan already there, sporting bandages and looking shaken, but otherwise unharmed. "Now rest here with your friends. The Doctor will be with you momentarily."

The girls waited for the Madame to depart and then turned to each other, joyful despite their injuries. "Hey, Abby," Megan smiled. "Glad you're okay, girl. That bitch said you got the worst of their 'treatment' 'cause of your little stunt the other day."

"It was horrible, but I got through it thanks to our . . ." Abby trailed off as the goon returned with her water. She thanked him without making eye-contact and waited for him to leave before continuing. "You know, our friend? It stayed with me while I was trapped in that box. It soothed me, made me feel safe."

"Me too!" Megan said. "They hung me from the ceiling with this two-pronged fork thingy strapped around my throat. One end pointed under my chin, the other here"—she tapped her sternum—"so that I couldn't lower my head without impaling myself. Well, I started to panic. I mean, what if I fell asleep? Bye, bye, Megs, right?"

"And that's when the ghost came to you?" Abby asked, studying the bandage around Megan's throat. By the looks of it, she must have nodded off at some point before the piercing pain brought her screaming back to consciousness.

"Yeah, it just showed up, like it came right through the wall. I was scared at first, but, well, just being in its presence was soothing, you know?"

"Yeah," Summer said. "They put me in this cage and lowered me into a giant tub of ice water. My head was the only part of me still sticking out and only that by a few inches. The Doctor said that the cold would sap my strength until I couldn't stand any more. At which point, he said, I would drown. He left me there in the dark. I could already feel the cold numbing my skin. I figured it was only a matter of time before I went under."

"Weren't you scared?" Abby asked.

"Hell yes I was scared, but I also kind of accepted it. Maybe it's for the best, I told myself. At least it would be an end to all this torture bullshit. That's when I felt this . . . I don't know how to describe it . . . this other presence in the cage with me. It made me feel strong, you know? Helped me get through the experience."

"Wow, your punishments sound a lot worse than mine," Abby marveled. "Why'd they tell you mine was the worst?"

"Because ours only lasted a day," Summer said. "They wanted to break you because, no offense, but they consider you the weakest of us."

"They know we're up to something," Megan whispered. "They wanted you to rat us out."

Abby looked at the expressions on their faces and felt a blossom of anger. So, she was designated the 'weak one' was she? Well, just because she wasn't bone-headed like Megan or had a death wish like Summer didn't mean she was weak. She just had sense enough to see the utter hopelessness of their situation. Maybe they could escape if they worked together but it was far more likely that they would die here, and no one would ever know what became of them.

"I didn't tell them anything," Abby said. "The plan's still good but we better hurry it up because they might not ask us so nicely next time."

Summer offered a thin smile. "Okay, good. But we have to play it smart, okay? We'll watch our hosts, learn their movements. When it looks safe, we bust the hell out of here."

Chapter 7

Like with the first round of torture, the girls were allowed a short reprieve to heal from their wounds. They used their time wisely.

Over the next few days, they kept a close eye on the schedules of both the Madame and Doctor. They had no idea where they went when they weren't hanging out in the dungeon, so Megan had tried following them, hoping to find a way out. She had reached a dead end instead. If the wall contained a secret passage she couldn't find it. Their captors seemed to appear and disappear at their leisure.

None of the girls had the means of telling time—all such devices had been stripped from them when they first arrived—but they determined from what scant rays of external light pierced the dungeon's dingy hide that their captors were most active from the early hours of evening until the first light of dawn.

"So they're a bunch of night owls," Summer whispered as they ate dinner that night in the dining room. Like last time, they were served delectable meals along with as much alcohol as they wanted. Summer warned against drinking too much. Now more than ever they needed to keep their wits about them, but Megan and especially Abby opted to partake of the endless bottles of alcohol. According to Abby, they deserved to unwind a bit after all they'd been through.

"There's something strange about those two," Megan said. She paused with a glass of Merlot to her lips and added: "Other than the obvious, of course."

"I snuck into the kitchen the other night while they were in another part of the building," Summer said. "I was able to get hold of a knife. Don't ask me how, they usually keep the cutlery locked up tight, but there the knife was as if someone had left it out for me."

"They probably forgot to put it back," Abby slurred. She was on her third glass of Chardonnay. Summer didn't like her so tanked. The

Madame already had her pegged as the weakest link in their self-forged chain. So far, the girl had been able to resist their "questions," but alcohol had a way of loosening one's tongue, which was probably why their captors had allowed them to drink as much as they liked.

"I don't think so," Summer went on. "It's almost as if it was left there for me to find."

Megan giggled. "By our ghostly friend?"

"Maybe. But I was able to smuggle it back to my room. I'll try the infirmary tonight, see if I can't steal some needles and thread."

The other two nodded at this. They had to remove the tracking devices the Madame had implanted in them. That meant they would have to operate on each other. None of them were looking forward to the prospect of being cut open. One false move and they could be in serious trouble, but what other choice did they have?

"We'll shoot for tomorrow night," Summer said.

"About time," Megan agreed.

Abby laughed derisively. "Sooner we get this over with the better."

Summer caught her arm before she could take another sip of wine. "We're going to do this, Abby. With or without you. So, if you plan on coming you better lay off the sauce."

Abby pulled her arm free, sloshing wine all over the tablecloth. "Go ahead and leave me behind. I'm the weak one, remember?"

Summer yanked the glass from Abby's hand and shattered it against the wall.

"Oh, quit being a drama queen. You're just as strong as the rest of us. You spent three days in a freaking iron maiden for crying out loud."

"That's pretty tough," Megan interjected.

Abby covered her face with her hands and wept. "But I'm scared. God, I'm so scared."

"You think I'm not?" Summer pulled her hands free so she could look Abby in her tear-stained eyes. "We're all scared but we have to work together if we're going to get out of this. Do you understand? We have to have each other's backs!"

Abby sniffed and wiped at her eyes. "Yeah. Yeah, okay."

Summer continued to look the girl in her eyes. To Abby's credit, she didn't look away. "Do you have my back?"

"Yeah."

"Say it."

"I've got your back."

Without breaking eye-contact Summer said: "What about you, Megs?"

Megan scoffed. "You even gotta ask?"

"Okay." Summer took her napkin and wiped Abby's eyes for her. "Tomorrow night we put this place behind us, okay?"

The others agreed.

That night, Summer snuck from her room and made her way down the winding iron stairs to the infirmary. She wore a black robe she found in an old trunk in one of the rooms. Neither Madame or the Doctor seemed to object to her having it so she wore it whenever possible because it's pockets were large enough to store all the items she needed for their amateur operation.

Summer stuffed those pockets now with needles, bandages, tape, and thread. She grabbed a bottle of alcohol on the way out, considered, and took another for good measure. One they would use on their wounds, the other she would use to sanitize the knife. God only knew where that thing had been.

It occurred to her as she made her way back to her room that maybe they didn't really have tracking devices surgically implanted in them. She wasn't sure how someone would get their hands on such a piece of technology, but it couldn't be cheap. What if the Madame only told them she'd implanted them with the devices to ensure they obeyed her? On the other hand, if they were real then their captors could be keeping tabs on them right now, making all this sneaking around pointless.

Still, Summer had to risk it. She wasn't the type to timidly wait for the slaughterer's ax. If she was going to die then she'd die on her feet, screaming defiantly into that bitch Madame's face.

The next day was like any other. If their captors suspected them of being up to no good they didn't show it. Summer took that as a good sign. When she had her companions alone she told them that they would meet in her room tonight. She often watched her giant-screened TV with the volume cranked up, so they could use it to mask the sounds of their final preparations before they made their escape.

"Bring anything you think we'll need," Summer said. "Just remember we have to travel light."

"Do you think we'll really get out of here?" Abby asked. "I mean, what if . . . what if they catch us?"

"Then we'll be no worse off than we are now," Summer said.

"They're going to kill us no matter what," Megan said. "Do you think they're going to let us go after all this?"

Summer nodded in agreement. "At least this way we stand a chance."

"Okay." Abby called up whatever reserves of strength she had left in her. She offered her companions a strained but determined smile. "Let's do it."

They set their escape in motion that evening after dinner. The girls, wary now of the Madame's tricks, ate and drank very little of the sumptuous feast spread out before them even though they knew they needed to keep up their strength. They couldn't risk being drugged and waking up tied to a rack or some other bizarre torture device. This madness had to end, and it would end tonight, one way or another.

They met in Summer's room as planned. The Smiths belted "The Queen Is Dead" from the TV's speakers as the girls went over their inventory laid out on the bed. They had Summer's knife, the steel leg from Megan's bed, the supplies taken from the infirmary, several candles, a box of matches, and a couple of soft, cotton robes Abby had scrounged from her walk-in closet. There was no sign of their unpleasant hosts, and they could only assume they were asleep.

"Guess we best get to it," Summer said.

"Yeah," Abby and Megan said at the same time. None of them were keen on the idea of cutting each other open but a little pain now beat the hell out of another torture session in the dungeon.

Summer gathered the medical supplies and they sat near one another on the floor. Summer made sure to keep the bedroom door in her line of sight. The last thing they needed was the Madame or that sadistic boyfriend of her's popping in on them unannounced.

They hyped each other up for the small incisions. Summer went first and Abby held her hand. Megan took the knife and cut across the healing scar on Summer's stomach. Summer gritted her teeth and tried not to cry out. Megan got the chip out and then put it on the ground next to them. She sewed Summer back up pretty easily. It looked messy, but the job was done.

Megan went next and Abby held her hand too. Summer cut across Megan's arm where her scar was. Megan groaned with discomfort and Summer pulled the chip out, and laid it next to them. Then she sewed Megan's arm back up. Abby went last. Summer was a bit more recovered than Megan, whose right arm now was useless, so Summer performed the operation. Megan was glad too. Cutting Summer's belly open had been a scary prospect and it was all she could do to keep her hands from shaking. Summer seemed a bit more at ease with it. Megan watched as she cut across Abby's back where the incision had been made and pried out the chip. Abby cried out and Megan clasped her hand over the girl's mouth to help stifle the sound.

"What do we do with them?" Abby said, nodding to the chips.

"We leave them here," Summer suggested. "With any luck, that bitch will think we're still in our rooms."

"Sure, but what if we run into that goon of theirs?" Megan said.

Summer wiped blood from the edge of her knife. "I guess it's a good thing that I got in some practice with this."

Abby groaned and looked away. Megan grinned and shot Summer a wink.

The girls made their way deep into the building's bowels. They were all feeling weak from their minor surgery, but knew there was no time to rest and lick their wounds. They had to stay strong and get out of here before their captors found them missing.

They tiptoed down the hallway leading to the torture rooms. As before, they had trouble finding the right room, and, as before, their shadowy friend appeared to show them the way. They stepped into the room containing the grate.

"We did it," Abby gasped.

"We're not free yet," Summer said. "Come on, Megs, we gotta hurry."

"Don't have to tell me twice." Megan and Summer removed the grate and got to work chipping away the remainder of cement. Abby watched the door and tried to keep the candle in her hand from shaking too badly. She didn't want it going out, not this close to freedom.

It took them less than half an hour before the hole was wide enough for them to slip through.

Summer peered into the darkness below. "We don't know what's down there. I'll go first."

"Be my guest," Megan said.

Summer snorted. "Geez, don't try to stop me or anything." She sat on the edge of the hole and forced a smile. "See you on the other side." She disappeared into the blackness.

Abby and Megan waited with baited breath until they heard Summer call up to them: "What're you waiting for? Come on!"

The two girls hugged each other and then squeezed through the opening one at a time. Megan was the last in. She paused long enough to give the place a one finger salute. They'd get out of here and find some adults. Once they explained what happened here they'd come back with the police and, if she had her way, they'd burn this wretched place to the ground.

The sewer's tunnels were vast, dark, and riddled with passages that branched off in every conceivable direction. The girls walked in circles, trying to keep to the walkways and out of the sewage, which stank so bad they had to use their robes to cover the lower parts of their faces.

There were sounds in the tunnels, what seemed like footsteps and the occasional *sploosh* as something crawled into the wastewater. They didn't bother to investigate the sounds. Whatever haunted these sewers could keep to themselves. As far as they were concerned, the quicker they found a way out the better.

"We're lost," Abby moaned as she recognized a section of tunnel they had passed by twice already.

"We have to keep going," Summer panted.

"Go where?" Megan said. "We must've walked for hours now."

Summer shined her candle along the wall. Each of them carried one, having used the spares Summer brought along in her cloak. "There has to be a ladder or something. Keep looking."

There was a splashing sound behind them. Megan turned and shone her light on the wastewater just as something disappeared under it, leaving ripples on the murky surface. "Uh, guys, we might want to get a move on."

"Look!" Abby pointed to a section of wall lit up by their candles. Their shadowy friend was back, its amorphous form swirling to and fro as if beckoning them to follow. They did so without hesitation. They wanted to run but knew they shouldn't for fear of making too much noise. Whatever Megan had seen in the water might have no interest in them, but they didn't want to take any chances. They walked briskly instead, still following the ghostly shadow. It led them down a few twisted passages until they at last reached a ladder leading up to a manhole cover.

"Are we strong enough to push that lid aside?" Summer asked.

"Sure, if we put all our strength behind it," Megan said confidently.

Another splash sounded behind them. Summer dropped her candle and began up the ladder. "Get the lead out!" she whispered.

Abby dropped her candle and followed behind her. Megan was last. She raised the candle, hoping for a glimpse of whatever was following them. She got more then she bargained for as she saw a pair of red eyes coming right at her. Megan screamed and swiped her candle at the thing in a futile attempt to ward it off.

The Madame's sweetly cruel voice sounded in her head:

"You've been a naughty girl."

Then the Doctor's voice, so clear that he could've been standing beside her:

"Are you tired of our hospitality already?"

"You can't escape us that easily."

"The punishments will continue."

"We have such wonderful plans for you all."

The sewer-dweller closed in on Megan. She shook the voices from her head and raised the candle in a defensive gesture. Whatever the thing was it would have had her if not for the intervention of their shadowy friend. It appeared between the thing and Megan and expanded until it seemed to fill the entire passage.

"Run!" a girl's voice sounded faintly from the darkness. Megan didn't have to be told twice. She leapt onto the ladder and would have barreled right past the two girls had they not already braced themselves at the top. Both Summer and Abby had one foot planted against the sewer wall and the other on the top rung of the ladder while they pushed against the manhole cover with both hands.

"Help us," Summer grunted. Megan, her adrenaline in overdrive, laid into the cover with the force of a linebacker going for a tackle.

Together they moved the lid to one side and crawled out into the blessed night air.

Something let out a strangled cry from the sewer beneath them. They didn't wait to see if it would follow them up. The girls found their feet and ran as fast as their legs could carry them.

Chapter 8

It was pitch black outside. Thick woods threaded the edges of a vast field ahead of them. They realized with some trepidation that their captors had to know they were gone by now. Summer wondered if they would come looking for them. And if they did, how well did they know these woods? Were there traps laid out for the occasional stray child silly enough to think she could escape?

Summer dismissed the thought. It wouldn't do any good to dwell on what she had no control over. All that mattered was finding someone who could help them.

They held hands as they ran into the woods. Summer took the lead with Abby bringing up the rear. They didn't stop running until they stumbled across a narrow road. The girls followed the road, making sure to stay near the edge of the woods in case their former captors came looking for them.

Summer had them hide along the embankment when they saw headlights appear in the distance. "It could be the Madame's goon," she said.

"Yeah, but what if it's not?" Megan said. "Could just as easily be somebody driving home from work and we'll miss our chance."

"But what if it's them?" Abby crouched lower in the grass as she watched the headlights grow closer.

Megan shrugged her shoulders. "We'll have to chance it."

"Absolutely not," Summer said.

The car was almost upon them, its headlights blotting out all but its most basic shape. They saw that it was a large vehicle, possibly a van, and that meant that they had a fifty-fifty chance of it being the white van that had been used to capture them all. But what if it wasn't? Stranded out here as they were, it was only a matter of time before they were recaptured. If they didn't find a ride and soon then they were done for.

"I've gotta risk it," Megan said. "You two stay here, if it's that bitch's lackey then run like hell. Don't worry about me."

"Megan, no," Summer said, but the girl was already on her feet, flagging the car down. Summer and Abby held their breath as the vehicle slowed and then came to a stop. They saw it was a gray Buick minivan and let out a collective sigh.

Megan cautiously approached the driver side window and spoke with someone inside. She smiled and waved to her companions who likewise approached the minivan with wary curiosity. They hadn't come this far just to get captured all over again. However, their fears were quickly quashed when they saw the elderly couple in the front seat. "Please, we need help," Summer pleaded. "These crazy people, they kidnapped us! They . . . they did horrible things to us! Please, help us!"

"Now just slow down," the elderly woman said. "You kids get in the back and we can talk on the way."

The three of them all but leapt into the backseat of the minivan and Megan yelled for them to go. "Where exactly are you wanting to go?" the elderly man asked.

"Police station," Summer panted. "We need to speak with the police."

"Sure, it's just four miles away, but would you mind telling us what happened?"

"Please, just hurry," Summer said.

The couple took turns asking them questions but the girls told them that they didn't want to discuss the matter and then just stopped talking altogether. Abby stared out the back window at the receding tree line. She could've sworn she heard a rage-filled scream somewhere in the distance.

The elderly couple dropped them off at a police station just outside of Pittsburgh, Pennsylvania. Summer examined the building, taking in every detail of the brick and mortar as if to assure herself it was really there. She had never felt so relieved in her life. She turned back to the car, meaning to ask the elderly couple if they would come inside with them, but the car was gone.

Had the couple decided they didn't want to involve themselves any more than they already had? Summer shrugged. It didn't matter. They'd done enough just bringing them here. She offered her companions a thin smile and extended her hands. "Everyone ready?"

The girls smiled back, Abby a little shakily. They each took a hand and, as one, entered the police station.

A lieutenant named Bill Houghton approached them the moment they stepped inside. He saw the state they were in and began bombarding them with questions.

The girls told him that they needed to make sure they were safe before they spoke to him because they were afraid of reprisals from their captors. They also made the Lieutenant promise that he wouldn't separate them. He assured them that there was nowhere safer than a police station and then had a colleague fetch the girls some hot cocoa while he took them into his office, so they could tell him their story.

They spent the better part of an hour reliving the horrors of their captivity. Houghton jotted down every detail in his notebook, had an assistant bring the girls more cocoa, and had them go over the story several more times for clarification. Megan grew restless and lost her cool, shouting at the Lieutenant that they were wasting time sitting here. "Those kooks could be getting away right now! You've got to stop them!"

Houghton sat back in his chair with a sigh. "You're right, of course. The problem is, the place you've described, it sounds like the old Reverie mental hospital, but that place shut down back in the early sixties."

"That must be it," Summer said. "Please, you have to go there now and arrest them before it's too late."

"What I'm going to do, young lady, is send you girls to a hospital to get your wounds looked after, then we're going to call your parents, let them know you're okay. How's that sound?"

"No!" Abby shot to her feet, her face a mask of barely contained fear. "You have to go out there, Lieutenant. Please, my injuries aren't that bad. I can show you where we escaped from. Please, we're not crazy."

Houghton let out another sigh. "Okay. You other two, you're going straight to the hospital, no questions asked." He looked at Abby. "And you, right after you show me where exactly you escaped from, you'll join your friends, okay?"

Abby nodded. "Yes, sir. Thank you."

"What do you need Abby for?" Megan asked. "Why don't you just go to the mental hospital if you know where it is?"

"Because Reverie was torn down fifteen years ago," Houghton said. "It was right after they found the bones of a bunch of missing children scattered throughout the place."

"The Madame," Summer gasped.

"I don't know about some Madame, but we did nab the killer. A guy named Bruce Spinster. Big guy. Got caught 'cause he used the same white van at each of the kidnappings. He used to be the caretaker at the hospital. Said he heard voices telling him to sacrifice the children. He went to the gas chamber a few years back. Couldn't've happened to a nicer fella."

The girls looked at each other. "The van," Megan mouthed. Summer shook her head for Megan to keep silent. This whole thing was weird enough without them mentioning that Spinster might be the same guy who kidnapped them in broad daylight. But how was that possible if he was already dead? Could it have been his . . . ?

Summer couldn't finish the thought. It was too damn creepy.

Once he had seen Summer and Megan off to the hospital, Houghton took two squad cars out to the spot where Abby believed the elderly couple picked them up. "We'll take it from here," he said to the girl. Abby began to protest but he stopped her. "You've been very brave taking us this far, but your part in this is done, understand? Now go be with your

friends, we'll take it from here."

Houghton waited until Abby was safely away in one of the squad cars and then proceeded on foot through the dense copse of trees with two officers, Smith and Pierson, following close behind. Houghton didn't expect to find anything, but he had to at least check out the girls' story before he wrote it off.

It was Pierson who found the entrance to the sewers, right where the girls said it would be. "We're not going down there are we, Lieutenant?" he asked in a tone that pleaded for the answer to be no.

"Don't get your panties in a bunch," Houghton said as he descended the ladder. The two officers gave each other a despondent look and followed.

They made their way through the twisting maze of tunnels, their guns in one hand and flashlights in the other. All was silent around them. *Dead silent,* Houghton thought. He didn't like it. These tunnels obviously connected to the old hospital, what he and his friends had called "the Devil's Dungeon" due to a string of murders that had taken place there back in the 1960's. Murders performed by a crazed doctor and his nurse/lover. The incident had led to the place being shut down soon after, but the doctor and his lover disappeared. Police never were able to find them and to this day they were high on their most wanted list.

After the Spinster murders in the early 2000's, he had led the petition to tear the building down. He would've had the place sown with salt as well had he been allowed. There was something off about the grounds where the hospital once stood. He couldn't explain it, just that it felt like a sickness of some kind. If a place could be sick, that is.

He was so lost in thought that he nearly jumped out of his skin when Smith called to him. Houghton laughed at himself and looked at what the officer had found. It was a grate hanging open in the ceiling about six feet above them. Houghton, the tallest of the three, was able to reach up and grab hold of the grate. Smith and Pierson gave him a boost and he squeezed through into the room above. It was a tight fit, but he was as skinny as he was tall and managed with an inch or two to spare.

Once inside, he helped Smith up. Pierson, who was too round to fit through the tight opening, was ordered to go back and wait by the car. He did so gladly. Houghton and Smith found themselves in the dungeon-like room the girls had described. The iron maiden, the torture table, all the implements that mankind used to inflict suffering on their fellow man (or, in this case, girls) was here.

"Those poor kids," Smith said. The anger in his voice was unmistakable.

"Not so fast." Houghton shown his light on some of the torture devices. "Look how rusted everything is. This stuff hasn't been used in years."

"But what about the girls' wounds? They didn't get those falling off a slide. They were cut and beaten and sewn back together again."

"I know. None of this makes a lick of sense." Houghton made his way to the door, which had nearly corroded off its hinges, and opened it to reveal a narrow hallway that had caved in on itself long ago. "These rooms must be the lowest point of the old hospital, likely where they brought their most deranged patients for 'treatment'. When they tore down the building they must've either not known about this section or didn't care. Either way it amounts to the same thing."

"What's that, Lieutenant?"

"We're standing in a tomb."

Smith tried to suppress a shiver. "How the hell did those girls get in here?"

"Same way we did, most likely. You know kids, always going where they don't belong."

"But they said there was an infirmary, bedrooms, and a dining room. The way they described this place was that it was huge."

"Another thing kids are good at: exaggeration. Gotta give them points for creativity.

"So, do you think they were kidnapped?"

"I don't know. Probably. Those wounds didn't cause themselves. Maybe their kidnappers brought them here and they made up the whole thing about bedrooms big enough to go swimming in and what not just to keep sane."

Houghton froze as his flashlight framed something on the wall. At first, he thought it was just Smith's shadow, but that was impossible since the man was nowhere near the flashlight. The shadow moved about on the wall as if possessed with a mind of its own. What Houghton took for a head rose and turned in his direction, looking at him with eyes

that weren't there.

"What in the name of Christ," he managed to say.

The thing reached out for him with wispy black fingers. "Lieutenant!" Smith screamed. He grabbed Houghton by the arm and pulled him back towards the grate in the floor. Houghton got his feet moving and didn't spare the thing a backwards glance. Neither man had ever run faster from a place in their lives.

Abby, Summer, and Megan lay in the emergency ward. The officers who had escorted them made sure that their beds remained next to each other. This was done as much for the police's own benefit as for the girls' comfort. It would make it easier to keep tabs on them and ask them any follow up questions once Houghton returned.

The physicians put them on IV fluids for dehydration and had their wounds checked and treated. A psychiatrist was then brought in to diagnose their mental state. Though there seemed little doubt that the girls had been physically assaulted, their stories about maze-like dungeons, a crazed doctor with a half-melted face, and some ghost-like creature were a little hard to swallow.

"But it's true! All of it!" Summer pleaded.

"Of course, dear, please relax," the psychiatrist said. "What I don't understand is—"

"Don't call me 'dear'! That's what *she* called me!"

"Okay, okay, if you'll just relax."

"Why don't you leave us alone?" Megan cried. "Can't you see we've been through hell?"

"Yes, I see that, but the fact of the matter is that we have no evidence to back up these claims. Is there anyone else who can verify your story? An adult, perhaps?"

"I can attest to its authenticity." Houghton appeared in the ward, flanked by a discomposed Smith and Pierson. He dismissed the psychiatrist and nurses and had his men keep watch while he spoke privately with the girls. They immediately bombarded him with questions. Did he find the place? Was the Madame and her assistants there? Did he arrest them?

Houghton held up his hands for silence and, once he had it, said: "The place was torn down just as I told you, but I did find its lower section intact. The torture devices were there like you described, but there was no way you would have access to the rooms on the upper level because the place had none. I don't know what you thought you saw, but it's impossible."

"But we did see it!" Megan shouted. "Why won't anybody believe us?"

"It could've been mass hysteria brought on by your shared predicament," Houghton said. He saw the look of hopelessness on the girls' faces and added: "On the other hand, maybe . . . just maybe you three experienced a paranormal event. Something not of this world."

The three girls looked at each other. Summer smiled slightly and nodded. "Yeah, maybe. Strange that the weirdest shit would sound the most logical, right?"

Houghton returned the smile. "Yeah. You girls should rest. Your parents have been notified and they're already on their way. This place is tightly guarded, you don't have to worry about being . . . well, taken again."

The Lieutenant rose and began to leave but Abby called to him. "Sir? You saw something out there, didn't you? Something that changed your mind about us."

"Did you?" Summer sat up in bed. "What did you see?"

Houghton cleared his throat. "I met your shadowy friend. I think it wanted me to say hi."

"And there was nobody else there?" Summer pressed. "You're sure about that?"

"Believe me, I would've seen them if they were there." Houghton waved farewell and left the three girls alone.

"How can there be nobody there?" Megan asked.

"Yeah," Abby said. "We just escaped a few hours ago. How could they just disappear like that? I mean, you know, without a trace?"

"I don't know," Summer admitted. "I guess it depends on what we're dealing with, right?"

They all three shared the same thought, though none was brave enough to say it out loud. Just what were they dealing with here? Something outside of the norm, that was for sure.

Epilogue-1964

Helena woke to find herself lying on some sort of metal table. The last thing she remembered was entering the strange room in the catacombs deep under the mysterious cabin. She had run into a tall man dressed in a black tuxedo. He had grabbed her and shoved a cloth in her face. She had grown woozy and . . . and here she was, resting in what looked like a doctor's office. At least, that's what she figured it was. The place had all sorts of things on the shelves that looked like pharmaceuticals.

Was she at the Reverie mental hospital? She remembered wondering if the passages she was following led under the place but that couldn't be. The place was shut down after all those patients were murdered a while back. Of course, that didn't mean the people who did the murders couldn't return to the scene of the crime.

Helena jumped up and rummaged through the drawers that lined the room. She needed to find a weapon. She didn't know who the man was who had kidnapped her nor why he had brought her here—wherever *here* was—but she wasn't going to let herself be caught again so easily. She had to find something to defend herself with.

Helena found a scalpel in one of the drawers, tucked it up her sleeve, and hurried back to the table just as she heard the door open. A woman with crazy red hair entered along with the tall man, who was now wearing a doctor's smock. "See?" the man said, grinning, "young, just like I told you."

"Yes, yes," the woman said. Then, to Helena: "Hello, dear, how are you feeling? Come with us, we have a special room prepared for you."

"Where am I?" Helena asked. "Who are you people? What do you want with me?"

"You'll find out soon enough," the lady said. "But from here on out you will address me as 'Madame', are we clear?"

"I don't—"

"Are we clear?"

Helena let out an agitated sigh. "Yes, Madame."

"Good. Now come along, we have such wonderful things planned for you."

Helena decided to play it cool. She followed the Madame and the guy who looked like a doctor out of the room. They took her down a hallway to another section of this enormous subterranean castle. But how could a castle be underground? Helena wondered. She had no time to dwell on the subject. They stopped in front of a door at the far end of the hallway and the Madame herded Helena inside.

This room was larger than the other with a metal table in one corner, a rectangular box big enough to hold a human inside in another, and a claw-foot tub set against the far wall. Helena felt her stomach do a somersault. Something was very wrong here. "What is this place?" she heard herself ask.

"What is this place . . . what?"

"What is this place, Madame?"

"Oh, it's neither here nor there," the Madame crooned. "Now be a good girl and have a seat. We shan't be long."

The Madame and Doctor locked the door behind them as they left.

Helena clutched her shoulders and allowed the shiver she had been repressing to work its way through her body. Okay, seriously, what the hell? She had never been so afraid. What did these cuckoos want with her? Just how much trouble was she in?

She found a small place underneath the metal table to hide the scalpel in case she needed it later. After that, she took in her surroundings. She got an up-close look at the metal human container, which was locked up tight. Probably for the best, she thought. Let it stay locked. She wasn't that eager to find out what the inside looked like. She checked out the claw-foot tub next, noting the red stains around its porcelain rim. If those stains were what she thought they were, then she was in more trouble than she dared believe.

She heard the door unlock, and the Madame entered with her minion in tow. She carried a coil of rope in her hands, he held a metal tray containing various medical instruments and a glass bottle in both of his.

"Up on the table," the Madame ordered.

"Why?" Helena managed to say. She was so nervous she could barely keep her teeth from chattering.

The Madame offered a placating smile. "So that we can tie you up, of course."

"Why?" Helena managed again.

"Because you are to be our first experiment," the Doctor chimed in.

"Isn't that wonderful?" the Madame beamed. "And who knows, if things work out with you then maybe we'll pluck more fresh lilies from the field."

The Doctor laughed. "There's no shortage, that's for sure."

"You're not coming anywhere near me!" Helena backed towards the table. Too late she realized the folly of hiding the scalpel. She should have kept it on her, but she hadn't been thinking clearly. She supposed she hadn't wanted to get in trouble if they caught her with it. Now she would have to make a dash for the blade and pray she could reach it before they stopped her.

The Madame shook her head. "Oh dear, looks like we have a troublemaker."

"Well, we'll just have to teach her her place." The Doctor sat the tray down on the table and grabbed Helena by the front of her shirt.

"Let go of me!" Helena screamed.

"Once we have you tied up nice and secure," the Madame said, raising the rope.

Helena's flailing hand grasped the glass bottle on the tray. She caught only a glimpse of the bottle's description as she broke it over the Doctor's head, but that was enough to give her hope. The label read: SULPHURIC ACID.

The Doctor let go of her at once as he clutched at his burning face. The sound of his skin sizzling as the acid ate through it was horrifying, but a small part of her delighted in his pain. It was no less than what he had planned for her, she was sure.

"You little brat!" the Madame shouted.

Helena was small but spry. She dodged the Madame's grasping hands and scrambled for the scalpel hidden under the table's rear right leg. Behind her she heard the Doctor howling in pain. It drowned out the Madame's own shouts. Helena had to find the scalpel quickly. Where was it? The place was so dark. She could barely see her hand in front of her—there it is!

Pale light from the single bulb hanging overhead reflected off the blade's surface. Helena lunged for it just as the Madame grabbed for her. "Got you now!" she snarled. She caught Helena by her hair and twisted until the girl thought her whole scalp would come off. Tears welled in her eyes, but Helena continued to paw for the scalpel.

"Such naughty children must be punished," the Madame said. "Oh yes, you will pay dearly for this outburst. Your death shall come in increments!"

Helena's fingers slid across the scalpel's handle. Without thinking, she slashed at the fingers that were dug into her scalp like talons. The Madame hissed and let go of Helena's hair. The girl fought to regain her feet. The Madame wiped her bloody hand on her dress and then produced a knife of her own from one of its pockets. "Oh, you bad girl! I'm going to put you in the box and leave you there to rot!"

"No way, I've had enough of you!"

The two made a sweeping stab at each other. Helena felt the Madame's blade sink into her stomach just below her ribs. Her scalpel pierced the woman's heart. Both fell to the floor, the Madame in an inanimate heap, Helena in the fetal position, clutching her stomach and moaning in pain as her life blood slowly trickled out of her.

Helena couldn't believe how much pain she was in. She had been stabbed in the stomach. She'd read somewhere that it took a long time to die from a stomach wound. She would probably lay here in agony on this cold floor for a long time before she finally expired. She looked at the Madame's body lying a few feet away. At least she was able to kill her before she died. She was seriously done with that bitch.

The Madame's body twitched. Helena drew in a gasp that caused hot springs of pain to erupt through her stomach. The body moved and then a hand reached over it, searching for Madame's knife. The Doctor's head appeared next. His face looked half-melted and he was blind in one eye. The other had melted from its socket. "Where are you, you little cunt!" he

wheezed. His words came out in a gurgle, as if his throat was filled with blood. His hand found her foot and he shouted in triumph. "There you are! Come here!"

Helena kicked at him but to no avail. She was too weak from loss of blood. The Doctor began to crawl over the Madame, his one sightless eye rolled back and forth in its socket as it futilely tried to draw a bead on her. "Where—" he began but Helena stabbed him in the throat with the scalpel before he could finish. The Doctor clawed at his throat, gurgled one last time, and collapsed on top of the Madame.

Good riddance, Helena thought weakly. It was getting more difficult for her to breath. After a long few minutes, Helena felt herself drifting away. She looked around the room as best she could. All the objects began to blur together and, right before she took her last breath, she thought she saw the Madame and Doctor standing over her.

No, she thought, I killed you. That's impossible. There's no coming back from death. That's impossible . . . isn't it?

A moment later, Helena also drifted into death.

To this day the three of them are said to haunt the dungeon where the Reverie mental hospital once stood. Two malevolent spirits reported to resemble a red-haired woman, a doctor with a half-melted face, and a shadowy spirit that sometimes took the form of a young girl. It is believed that the "Doctor" and "Madame", as they are called, continued their dreams of kidnapping adolescents for their own nefarious purposes, though it is also said that the shadowy spirit of the young girl will often help those who fall victim to the evils inherent to that cursed place.

A place that the locals would forever after refer to as the Devil's Dungeon.

Don't miss out!

Visit the website below and you can sign up to receive emails whenever Cassie Smith publishes a new book. There's no charge and no obligation.

https://books2read.com/r/B-A-VZKAB-YTVOC

BOOKS 2 READ

Connecting independent readers to independent writers.

About the Author

Cassie Smith grew up in Indiana and has always wanted to be a writer. As a child, she would write stories all the time for her parents. Cassie lives with her spouse and child in Indiana.

Read more at https://www.amazon.com/stores/author/B0CCSVGZY5/about.